"You seduced me," Parnell accused.

He sounded so lachrymose, Rebecca realized it was going to take him some time to come to grips with his emotions. He'd have to find out for himself that warring against fate was a losing battle.

"Funny, isn't it?" she said. "How you're only now complaining?" Despite his gloom he hadn't yet loosened his hold on her.

"We can't let this go one bit further. You might as well know, I'm a coward. All I want to do is fly."

"You sure had me soaring."

"I did?" He tripped over his ego. "I mean, so what?"

"So, nothing. We don't have to do this ever again." She slid her hand from his chest to his thigh. But before he could do more than groan, she moved away.

Parnell s̶a̶ _____ ressing hand had _____ e," he said.

"I'm not. _____ es."

"I hate women who do that."

For **Jackie Weger**, writing romances is a way to put magic in her life. Having had five children before the age of twenty-two, she suspects she missed out in the fantasy department. It wasn't until she was forty that Jackie experienced the joy of unleashing her creative energy, writing her first novel in only three weeks. She did slow down considerably after that, taking time to do on-site research for all the ten Harlequins that followed. Jackie and her husband, H.A., now enjoy an empty nest in Alabama.

Books by Jackie Weger

HARLEQUIN TEMPTATION

89—THE WINGS OF MORNING
159—THE WAY OF DESTINY
181—EYE OF THE BEHOLDER

HARLEQUIN AMERICAN ROMANCE

5—A STRONG AND TENDER THREAD
48—COUNT THE ROSES

HARLEQUIN SUPERROMANCE

227—BEYOND FATE

On a Wing and a Prayer

JACKIE WEGER

Harlequin Books

TORONTO • NEW YORK • LONDON
AMSTERDAM • PARIS • SYDNEY • HAMBURG
STOCKHOLM • ATHENS • TOKYO • MILAN

Published June 1988

ISBN 0-373-25307-9

Printed in U.S.A.

1

"SANTEE, YOU HANG ON to Nicholas," Rebecca ordered as she lined up the five orphans just inside the hangar door. She had an instant sensation of space and unfamiliar shadow. The building, huge and poorly lit and smelling of grease, much like a mechanic's garage, intensified the sensation. Rebecca shivered. She'd had misgivings about this trip from the start, but her arguments against it had fallen on deaf ears. In her heart she felt the children would end up being disappointed yet again. Too, she wasn't certain of her ability to handle the five on her own. The orphans seemed to have an instant affinity for troublemaking.

"I'm hungry," said Jonesy. "We should've stopped at McDonald's for breakfast."

"They aren't open this early, it's barely dawn. Besides, you had breakfast."

"I'm cold," said Yancy.

"Swing your arms. I'll be right back. Don't anybody wander off. And hang onto your totes—I mean it. I'll go find the office."

It really wasn't much warmer inside the monolithic Quonset than outside, but at least they were out of the wind and sleet, thought Rebecca. She turned and studied the shadows.

She could make out the nose and propeller of a small plane and what seemed to be the dismantled parts of another. At the far end a beacon of light slanted from a pair of windows. She admonished the children once again not to wander, then negotiated the length of the building.

She stopped in the beacon of light and stared through the dusty windows.

As her brain registered the airline office her disquiet grew. There were furnishings of every kind that had nothing in common with each other but their infirmity and a dusty, dilapidated air. An oil heater was turned so low it had no effect on the thick rime of frost at the outside windows, where the curtain rods were bent and barely hanging on.

Amid all the clutter a man sprawled in a chair, asleep. His head was tilted back revealing a jaw covered with beard stubble, several days thick. His arms were folded across his chest and his booted feet were crossed and propped on the desk. He looked like a scruffy bag of assorted human parts loosely held together by army-surplus specials. He was a living reproach to manhood, Rebecca thought uncharitably. But then, she was intolerant of men. There wasn't a man in her life and she wasn't anxious to include one. If it meant lonely nights, well . . . her days were full.

But it saddened her that this was what the foundering Tynan Foundation had come down to; begging favors for the children from those who appeared least able to afford them. If she had one whit of sense, she'd grab up the kids, return to the orphanage and tell the director they'd missed the plane. She could practice the lie all the way back to Boise, then perhaps it wouldn't show on her face.

A yelp echoed in the dark vastness. She glanced at the orphans. They were arguing among themselves already. She expelled a sigh. They would put the rout to any lie about missing the plane. With a sinking feeling, she tapped hard on the metal door and moved across the threshold.

The man opened his eyes. Rebecca could see him trying to shake the dregs of sleep. Once his gaze seemed focused on her, she spoke, "I'm looking for Mr. Stillman."

He came alert, his lips thinning as suspicious eyes darted to appraise her.

"You a bill collector?"

"Rebecca Hollis, from the Tynan Foundation. Abigail Tynan booked us a flight on the mail run. To San Francisco," she added, since the man looked blank. "We're a bit early, but if you could just direct me to Mr. Stillman, I can let him know we're here."

"Captain Stillman."

"Captain Stillman, then."

The man dragged his feet from the desk, stood and stretched, which had the effect of making his shirt collar poke up like limp flags from beneath the crew neck of a British commando sweater. When he came out of the stretch, the gleam in his eye was still guarded. "You're looking at him and, I'm not."

"But . . ." Rebecca began. She caught herself before she blurted that he couldn't possibly be the pilot. She took a step back. Standing, the man was taller than she'd supposed. And given the slothful way his clothes hung on his frame, he appeared even more disreputable. The kind of man one either crossed the street to avoid, or if one were kind, dropped a quarter into his cup.

"You're not what?" she said, in no mood for benevolence, telling herself she'd misunderstood him.

"Not expecting you."

"You can't be Captain Stillman then, I assure you, we're expected." She was in no humor for charades. She'd spent the better part of last evening packing, managing only several hours' rest before she'd had to roust the children from their beds, after which she'd spent a tension-filled ninety minutes on slick and unsafe roads to reach the airfield on time.

"You hard of hearing or something? I'm Stillman." He was fully awake now. Irritably so. There was only the woman, but she was talking in plurals.

"We. Who's we?" he demanded.

Rebecca answered his hostility with what she considered to be more pleasantness than the situation required. "Myself, and the children. From the Foundation, the foundling home."

"Children!" Parnell Stillman yanked a clipboard from the wall behind him, flipping rapidly through it. "I got a group of social workers booked, going to a convention."

"I'm the social worker."

"There're six of you."

"One of me. Five children. I'm sure Abigail didn't say we were all social workers," ventured Rebecca. But she knew in her heart that the Foundation's director had probably misled the man with her use of sly and creative dialogue. When it came to bargaining, creative dialogue was Abigail Tynan's stock in trade. But bargaining with the likes of Stillman? Yes, Abigail would do that, too. She'd often said she'd bargain with the devil if it meant something good for the youngsters in her care.

Parnell Stillman consulted his notes. "Abigail said, 'important personages, big favor, cheap price.'" He remembered now. The old biddie had also reminded Parnell of her association with his Uncle Henry. "I wrote it down."

"Well, that's us," Rebecca said airily, offering a weak smile.

"Forget it. I'm not hauling you. That's final. No women or children. They make too much fuss. Everybody this side of the Continental Divide knows it. I don't even like being nice to women and children. Makes my stomach hurt. You can just take yourself out of here. Tell Abigail the deal's off."

It was just the out she was looking for. Now she could return to the Foundation and tell Abigail an honest truth—they'd been turned away, bumped from the flight. On the other hand, Rebecca thought indignantly, the pilot was being underhanded, unfair and rude. It made her mad. "I will not take myself out of here. You've been paid. You agreed." She hoped the check Abigail had sent hadn't bounced. Otherwise . . .

"I'll have my accountant send the Foundation a refund."

There was something in the way he said "my accountant." Rebecca eyed the stack of unopened mail on the desk, the disarray of paper in the In-Out basket, all of which was layered with undisturbed dust. Accountant, my foot, she thought. His tone held the same touch of superfluity that Abigail Tynan used in promising payments when she knew very well the Foundation's bank account was overdrawn. Rebecca knew just how to counter the pilot's maneuver.

"I'm afraid that won't do," she said. "We have to have the refund at once, in cash, so we can make other arrangements. It's urgent that we get to San Francisco."

"Can't. It's against my policy to give cash refunds. Besides, I don't keep cash on hand. Too dangerous. I might get robbed."

"You must not worry about getting robbed too much," Rebecca cooed, skepticism in full flower. "The gate at the entrance was open, your doors were unlocked. There's a plane sitting on the runway with no attendants that I could see. Security appears awfully lax. How many times have you been held up?"

Parnell scowled. The look she was giving him made him feel like something one scraped off a shoe. He didn't like it. "There's always a first time."

"No respectable burglar would be out in this weather," Rebecca said lightly. "Anyway, isn't there some sort of government rule that if passengers are bumped, the airline has to pay double the cost of their tickets?"

The belligerent expression on Parnell Stillman's unshaven face told Rebecca she'd hit a sore spot. "Who cares about government regulations? Paper pushers one and all," he sneered.

"You won't have to be nice to us, Captain Stillman. I wouldn't want to be the cause of inflaming your ulcers. The children and I are used to managing just fine without ordinary courtesies."

He glared at Rebecca, desperately intent. The way she talked reminded him of a bitter mistake he'd once made. "I had a wife like you once," he divulged, tight-jawed. "She spent the whole of our marriage intent on vexing me."

It was incredible, Rebecca thought, how full of himself the man was. She reminded him of his wife? Well, he reminded her of another who'd also been full of himself, shallow of heart and mind. A riposte came to the tip of her tongue, slid off with ease. "Oh? And how long did your marriage last, Captain Stillman. Twenty minutes?"

"Just like her," he muttered.

"I'm honored you think so," Rebecca replied so reverently her tone couldn't be taken for anything except what it was—unveiled sarcasm. She moved outside the office proper and called to the kids. Once they had all trooped the length of the hangar, she directed them to a bench along the inside office wall. "Sit there. Don't get up. You might—"

"I have to wee-wee," said Molly.

Rebecca's face flushed with chagrin. With no other source to ask, she had to direct the inquiry to Parnell. "Where's the ladies' room?"

Displaying ill-concealed annoyance, he pointed with a pencil, then sat down behind his desk and pretended his unwelcome passengers didn't exist. Though he did surreptitiously watch Rebecca remove her head scarf and overcoat. She looked young, vibrant, with her dark hair released, cascading in a froth about her shoulders. And much more shapely with her coat off. Much more. She was short, too. Women like her always tried to use that to advantage. Trying to make a man feel big, protective. Well, he didn't give a hoot in hell. A woman's shape, size and beauty no longer swayed him. They hadn't in years.

He knew all about womanly ploys—those provocative games of revealing a little here, a little there until a man was panting like a thirsty pup. He'd suffered the misfortune of becoming easy prey once. It would never happen again.

Back when he'd been stupid over women, he'd been in the Navy, stationed at the Pensacola Naval Air Station. The vamp that snagged him had made herself out to be a poor little widowed thing, all alone and with two darling children to raise. Just the memory of it made him sick to his stomach. He'd swallowed every honey-dripped word and married her. All she had done was raise one ruckus after another, and the darlings had turned out to be manipulative brats.

The marriage had spoiled the last three years of the twenty he'd spent in the Navy. At thirty-seven and at loose ends he'd made his way to Idaho where Uncle Henry had settled into crop dusting and hauling cargo. Two years ago Uncle Henry died. Parnell discovered the flying service had been bequeathed to him. The flying service and its mountain of debt.

What he needed, Parnell knew, was a sharp secretary-bookkeeper. But the salary he could offer wouldn't appeal to a man with a family to feed. That left hiring a woman and he couldn't make himself do it.

He counted himself among the honorable group of men who liked dogs, was kind to the elderly and had immense control over the needs of the flesh. Control was easy—his failed marriage had left him with a lingering animosity toward women. He didn't want anything in skirts hanging around the airfield. Secretary or passenger.

His self-imposed celibacy was annoying, but not earth shattering. On the infrequent occasions his flesh drove him to seek out a woman, he went where there was no romance, just bonhomie, crude jokes, loud laughter and inane conversation. If any woman mentioned marriage, he hightailed it on the double; if she mentioned kids, he disappeared faster than a jet stream in a howling wind. He protected himself from female wiles as best he could. His dimples had attracted the widow. Now he kept them concealed behind beard stubble. And he knew for a fact you couldn't be nice to a woman. First thing you knew she'd attach some unintentional sentiment to word or action. He had it in the back of his mind that women had been molded just to keep a man in misery. It was ironic that God had shorted men a rib just so he could create women. Parnell had decided long ago that he'd just as soon have his rib back.

His introspection was diverted to two of the boys edging crabwise off the bench. The control he had over his libido didn't extend to his disposition. He glared at them. "Get away from my desk."

"We're orphans," said Jonesy.

"Tough."

"What's he look like?" Nicholas whispered.

"Like that hobo old Abigail let sleep in the kitchen last week," Jonesy said.

"Hobo!" Parnell bristled. "Get back to that bench like you were told, you cheeky brat."

Jonesy didn't budge, but he kept a wary eye on Parnell. "Nicholas is blind," he volunteered. "He can't see nothin' but shadows."

"That's too bad," said Parnell, shocked and trying to sound mean. "I don't look like a hobo. I'm an aviator."

Nicholas squinted. "Can I feel your hands and face?"

"Hell no! Back up!"

Jonesy put a retraining arm around the younger boy. "We're goin' to San Francisco to see if we can get somebody to adopt us. There's a big meetin' with all these people who take handicapped kids."

Parnell's gaze took in Nicholas, Jonesy, and the two boys on the bench. Curiosity got the best of him. "What's wrong with you?" he asked Jonesy.

"I'm fat. Nobody wants a fat kid. Cost too much to feed."

"What about him?" Parnell nodded toward Yancy.

"He's got a friend named Scrappy."

"So?"

"Scrappy ain't real."

"Oh."

"Santee's got Indian blood. He won't stay in the city. Folks won't take him cause he runs away and lives in the woods. Molly has club feet. You got any kids?"

Parnell's curiosity dried up. "No, and I'm not looking to get any. Move out. Don't you know how to follow orders?"

"We've never been on an airplane before."

"I wish you weren't—" An idea flew into Parnell's brain. "Is that so? You scared to fly?"

Jonesy shrugged. Nicholas asked, "Is flying dangerous? What's it feel like?"

"It can be dangerous." Parnell's mouth compressed into the thinnest of smiles. "Yep, it sure can." The idea took solid root. He examined it from every direction and decided he had nothing to lose by trying it

on...on...he glanced at the manifest on the clipboard...Rebecca Hollis.

"Miss Hollis," he said as soon as she and Molly
emerged from the bathroom, "I need to go over the
flight with you." He unfolded a pair of charts, topographical and meteorological, over the clutter on his
desk. "It's a cold, bumpy ride. No frills, no food—"

"I know, we brought our own snacks."

Parnell withheld a sigh. "You're missing the point.
Look here. See this chart. This is the flight path from
Boise to San Francisco. We'll be flying over some of the
most desolate terrain in the country—"

"What does that matter? We're not walking."

Parnell dropped into his chair like a deflated bal-
loon. His idea wasn't working. He shot her his best
scowl. "That's true, but we got crosswind, maybe even
wind shear, sleet, snow. The weather isn't good—" Of
course he planned to dip down and fly south of it, but
he wasn't telling her that.

"Are you canceling the flight?"

"Can't. It's a mail run. You know the old saying,
'Neither rain nor sleet—'"

"If you feel it's safe enough to fly the mail..."

"I'm paid to take chances," Parnell said modestly.

"You were also paid to fly us to San Francisco. And
back."

All the curses he could think of glowered in Parnell's
dark eyes. "I don't want a woman and kids aboard my
plane. Women are a jinx! Kids are nothing but trouble."

Rebecca shooed Molly back to the bench, out of
earshot. She lowered her voice. "I'm sure you've been
told this before, Captain Stillman. You're acting like a

horse's rear end. I'm willing to accommodate you. Just refund double our money and we'll make arrangements elsewhere. The truth is, you don't look as if you could fly yourself out of a paper bag. It makes me nervous—"

Parnell's lithe frame went rigid. "You hoity-toity broad! What do you know about what flyers look like? I suckled in a cropduster, barnstormed at fourteen, flew jets at twenty-two. Lady, I was raised on a wing and a prayer in the literal sense. Don't look as if I could fly myself out of a paper bag! Maybe I ought to tell you what you don't look like."

"I didn't mean to insult you," Rebecca replied so sweetly it gave the lie to her words.

"You sure as hell did."

She glanced over at the children. One and all wore pensive expressions. The conclave in San Francisco meant hope. A hope of finding parents to love and be loved by in return. She couldn't take that away from the children. Even if it meant they had to tolerate an insufferable prig of a pilot. She turned back to Parnell and met his angry glare.

"All right, I did mean to insult you. I'm sorry. We'll just sit here quietly until it's time to board. If that's all right with you."

It wasn't, but Parnell knew when he was hoisted on a cleft stick. He knew it because he'd never been any other place in his life.

Flying was his freedom, flying ennobled his actions, and he was inseparable from it. But flying also distanced him from the business side of trying to run an airline single-handedly. Oh, he was a likable man when he wanted to be liked, usually when he was negotiating for freight or mail contracts, but he didn't like the paperwork. Somehow, when the money came in, it got spent in the wrong order. Like the fares from the Tynan Foundation which had gone to pay his relief pilot who had refused to climb into the cockpit yesterday until he'd had cash in hand.

He should never have let that old bat, Abigail, talk him into flying her "clients." But she'd once been a good friend of Uncle Henry's, bless his debt-ridden departed soul, and they'd done a fair amount of crop dusting for her before Abigail had sold off most of her land and turned what was left of her estate into a foundling home. Parnell eyed Rebecca with an expression longer than a mournful bloodhound's.

"I'll send one of the ground crew to tell you when to board. You'll have to carry your own luggage. Still-man's doesn't provide porters."

"We'll manage our own luggage. Thank you," Rebecca said, feigning congeniality.

Parnell shoved himself into a sheepskin jacket and stomped out of the office. They could hear his booted footsteps echoing long after he'd disappeared from sight.

"Bet he takes off without us," said Santee.

"Don't worry, he won't." Rebecca didn't know just how she knew that. Instinct, she supposed. Santee's olive complexion was pale. Afraid to fly, Rebecca knew, he was trying not to show his fear.

"He won't make me leave Scrappy behind, will he?" asked Yancy.

"Oh, I'm sure not. There'll always be room for Scrappy."

Rebecca wasn't supposed to encourage Yancy concerning the pretense of Scrappy even though Scrappy was Yancy's best friend. But everybody needed a best friend, she thought. It was a measure of her empathy that Yancy had been willing to introduce her to his imaginary playmate.

Each of the children had taken a hard blow, some more than one, which had taught them to keep a low profile, to keep heads tucked down, to harbor only meager expectations. In the year that she'd been working for Abigail Tynan, working with the children, they'd come to trust her, as much as they allowed themselves to trust any adult. To Rebecca's way of thinking, that trust was a measure of progress.

She gave a moment's thought to the conclave. Months of bickering, bureaucracy and red tape had gone into the planning of it. More than five different state agencies and a dozen private placement centers had pooled resources to bring it off. She hoped it worked. She hoped... She glanced at her charges... society's rejects—lame, blind, unloved.

A sudden whirlwind of memories and emotions whipped through her mind. Unloved. Perhaps, Rebecca thought, the reason she had such an affinity for the children was that she too was a reject.

But she had learned to love herself. No easy feat since she hadn't thought there was anything lovable about herself. And working with the orphans had filled some deep biological need.

Once the Foundation had found homes for these remaining five children though, Abigail was going to close its doors. Too bad, Rebecca thought, she couldn't find someone to adopt herself. As it was, after the first of the year she'd be on her own again. No job, no home, no kids.

No man in her life, either.

She didn't want a man, she reminded herself. Truth was, she'd been weakening on that score, especially in her dreams. Meeting the pilot strengthened her. He was a good representation of the opposite sex; arrogant, slothful, insensitive. She was always telling the children to let the past go, to learn to depend on themselves, accept reality. She needed to take her own advice.

Her thoughts ebbed, her gaze focusing on the present. Santee was beginning to fidget. Rebecca gave him an encouraging smile.

An elderly man, his wrinkled face pinched against the cold, entered the office. "You can git aboard, the cap'n says."

"Where's Captain Stillman?" Rebecca asked.

"Doin' preflight check."

"Well, here we go, kids. Our great adventure."

"Scrappy's afraid to get on a plane," said Yancy.

"He can go with me," offered Molly. "I'm not."

Yancy scowled. "He ain't that afraid."

"What's flyin' look like?" Nicholas wanted to know.

Rebecca sorted totes, handed them out and picked up her suitcase. "I'll describe it once we're doing it. Santee, guide Nicholas. Molly, Yancy, Jonesy, stay together."

The old man opened his mouth then closed it. Rebecca had the notion that he wanted to offer assistance, but had orders to the contrary. He gave an embarrassed nod and held opened the hangar door as she and the children filed out.

The tarmac was slick with crusted snow and ice, the wind and sleet shoving at them, taking their breath away. Landing lights guided their way. Just as she reached the foot of the gangway steps, Molly slipped, her balance undone by the heavy corrective shoes she wore.

Parnell, watching from the plane, sidled down the steps past the boys and snatched Molly, slinging her over his shoulder as he might a hundredweight sack of grain. "I'm not responsible for accidents," he yelled above the storm.

"Nobody said you were!" Rebecca yelled in return, exasperated and fighting to keep her own balance. From her shoulder perch Molly lifted her bonnet-covered head and grinned. She liked being the center of attention.

Unaware of Molly's delight, Parnell mumbled to himself. The flight was jinxed for certain, he thought. The kids would probably be airsick all over his plane.

Rebecca dragged herself, the suitcase and tote out of the stormy darkness. The old maintenance man—a frozen shadow—drove a forklift that would pull the loading ramp away from the plane. She shifted her gaze from the ghostly scene to Parnell. "Are you sure you can fly in this kind of weather?"

"You want to change your mind?" he said, all hope. "I'll have Amos—"

Rebecca pursed her lips. "If you're flying, we're flying."

"I gotta deliver the mail." With no snarl-ups, he thought. He'd landed a plum contract for December. Parcel post and the military APO San Francisco mail that was distributed to service personnel in the Pacific.

If he met the deadlines and kept his planes in the air, the money from the APO mail alone would pull his bottom line out of the red. He slid the door closed and secured it, then looked at Rebecca, at the ménage she had in tow. His stomach began to hurt. "Stow your gear," he said.

As he buckled himself into the pilot's seat, he decided he was going to stop being nice to elderly people. He'd been nice as pie to old Abigail Tynan and look at the trouble that officious, frumpy, octogenarian virago had bestowed on him. Soon as he got back from this run, he was going to buy himself a dog and be done with it.

That decided, Parnell preoccupied himself with what made him happy—flying airplanes. He scanned his flight plan and charts though he'd long since committed them to memory. The first engine turned over and sputtered to life, followed by the other three. He got the signal that the chocks holding the wheels were pulled. He released the brakes and shoved the four throttles against the stops. Then he aimed the nose into the blowing sleet and began rolling down the long ribbon of tarmac. Windshield wipers worked furiously, runway lights blurred past the wing tips, their luminescence fading behind the curtain of falling slush.

The weather didn't bother Parnell. He had the ability to fly through anything except solid mountain and he knew it. He expelled a satisfied smile. Flying was the high road.

2

"BUT YOU DON'T NEED a window seat, Nicholas," Jonesy argued. "You're blind! You can't see anything anyway!"

"I got here first!"

Rebecca jumped into the verbal fray. "Listen you two, you can take turns sitting by the window."

"But Nicholas could sit anywhere. It won't make any difference!"

"He has just as much right to a window seat as you do."

Jonesy sulked. "Everybody picks on me 'cause I'm fat."

"I don't!" cried Nicholas. "I can't see your old fat. I'm just takin' up for myself. Like I'm supposed to."

The plane shuddered, the boys quieted. Rebecca sighed. The plane staggered aloft.

The only light in the cabin was an eerie green glow spilling from the instrument panel in the cockpit, and the cold seemed to be seeping up from the steel deck. Rebecca pulled her coat collar up around her neck. Surely they weren't expected to suffer this debilitating cold the entire flight!

She was responsible for the safety and well-being of the children. What if they came down with the flu? A fever? And had to stay in bed during the conclave. It would break their hearts. Holding that thought, she kept her eye on Parnell, waiting for the right moment to approach him. Regardless of how cheap the fares, a little heat wasn't too much to ask.

The landing gear thumped loudly inside the wheel wells. The pilot was talking on the radio. When he seemed finished with the conversation, Rebecca got out of her seat and leaned into the cockpit. A welcome furl of warm air brushed her cheeks. It galled her that he was all nice and cozy while not giving a thought to the comfort of his passengers. She tapped him on the shoulder.

"Is there any way to give us some heat back here?" she asked, raising her voice above the harsh whine of the motors. "Our teeth are chattering."

Parnell twisted in his harness. He already knew the flight promised to be a rough one. Even the takeoff hadn't been exactly a garden-variety liftoff what with crosswinds and sleet bearing down on the overloaded plane. He wanted to concentrate on his flying, not pesky passengers. He displayed a mouth turned down in fixed antagonism. "Next you'll be asking when cocktails are served."

Hackles rose on the back of Rebecca's neck. She'd had her fill of the man's arrogance. "Look, all we've done is hire you to fly us to San Francisco. You're acting as if we're criminals or something. It's cold back here. And dark. A couple of the children are afraid of the dark."

"I'm a flyer, not a nursemaid," he said, but he touched a switch and a row of dim lights came on down the length of the ceiling throwing the children in the single row of seats and what appeared to be row upon row of carts stamped U.S. Mail into shadowy relief.

"Thank you," Rebecca said with unctuous civility. "Now, the heat?"

"You want heat? Open the vents next to the seats."

"Excuse me for disturbing you."

Suddenly there was a lurch of the aircraft. Rebecca fell to her knees. She grabbed the back of his seat and hung on.

She'd argued against attending the conclave and lost. She'd argued against flying. But the flux of December storms blanketing the West had finished that argument for her. The Foundation's old stationwagon was in too sad a shape anyway. Besides that, travel advisories had indicated that many of the main arteries were closed. She wished heartily that she had been more persuasive. Now there was nothing for it but to pray. A quick glance behind her revealed all the kids sitting straight and stiff, looking at her with frightened eyes from pale faces.

"Quit hanging on me and go sit down," Parnell shouted while his hands flew over the control panel.

"You're beyond belief!" she said, seething. But she managed to gain her feet and stumble back to the row of seats. Abigail must've been out of her mind when she booked their flight with Parnell Stillman! she thought crossly. In a brief moment of stability she found the heat vents, directing the warm jets of air across the seats.

"Ask him does he have parachutes," whispered Santee.

"Don't be silly," said Rebecca. "We're perfectly safe. I've flown on several occasions in worse weather than this." Not that she could think of one at the moment, but she did recall that the cabin attendants had always walked up and down the aisle reassuring passengers.

Sometimes the pilot got on the intercom and explained what was happening. It was obvious Captain Stillman had a passengers-be-damned! attitude. He wasn't going to explain a thing.

"Scrappy doesn't like flying," whimpered Yancy, clutching at his imaginary friend. "He's afraid he's gonna fall out of the sky."

"Well, he isn't and we aren't!" was said firmly to reassure herself as much as the children.

When finally the plane seemed to level out she turned her attention to passing out scrambled egg sandwiches.

The plane jerked, then began to slew sideways. For long seconds the engines sounded strained. They bounced, fell back, were buffeted severely. Screams erupted from the smaller children.

"You can have the window seat now, Jonesy," Nicholas wailed.

"Keep those brats quiet," the pilot shouted over his shoulder. "They sound like a bunch of banshees going to slaughter!"

Rebecca stared at the back of his head with defensive hostility. "Take us back to the airport!"

Parnell turned around and grinned. "Can't turn around, but I'll be glad to let you out at the next corner."

Rebecca listened to him laughing at his own joke. "You have a sick sense of humor."

By the time the engines sounded normal again, Molly had turned pale. Rebecca made her put her head down, cautioned the others to do the same if they too, felt ill. She continued to reassure them as best she could. She did this quickly, efficiently, lest the captain turn and again shriek some sarcastic remark at them.

Outside the windows the sky lightened from black to gray. They had a few minutes of smooth flight. One by one the children relaxed in the pale-gray hush and ate their sandwiches. Rebecca passed out juice, then opened her own thermos and sipped from it.

Parnell sniffed. He smelled coffee. He'd meant to grab a cup before he started preflight, but what with the hassle in the office, he'd forgotten. He took a quick look over his shoulder. The Hollis woman had a thermos. It stuck in his craw to ask, but—what the hell—the coffee smelled good. "Hey! Can you spare a cup of that?"

"Actually, no. But if you want to pull up to the next coffee shop," she replied sweetly, "we won't mind the delay."

He twisted around to face her. "Okay, I deserved that. We're even."

Rebecca opened her mouth to spew another rejoinder, but thought better of it. Why bring herself down to his uncouth level? Still, when she'd poured coffee into the lid that served as cup and handed it over his shoulder she had to say, "I'm not a stewardess, you know."

"You distracted me or I wouldn't have forgotten to grab myself a cup."

"You distracted yourself." She looked at the empty seat next to him. "Shouldn't a plane this size have a copilot? What if something happened to you?"

"You should've worried about that before you came aboard." He drained the cup, returned it to her. They hit another pocket of rough air. Used to it now, Rebecca placed a hand against the low ceiling and braced herself. Parnell tensed, manipulated the controls.

"Is something wrong?"

"Just turbulence, I warned you." His face clouded. The weather was more unstable than the forecast had predicted. And the plane was gathering weight. Amos had de-iced the wings, but Parnell could tell that ice was again forming on the plane. He was losing airspeed. He adjusted the power to compensate.

"You didn't really talk about danger," Rebecca accused. "You were trying to get us not to fly because you don't like us."

"Still don't," Parnell said, but his mind was on the worsening weather conditions. The storm front had leapfrogged down into the south-by-southwest course he'd plotted. Nature was never to be trusted and it had sure tricked him this time. A worried expression came over his face, which didn't go unnoticed by Rebecca.

"You're concerned aren't you? Can we go back. I mean that seriously."

Parnell shook his head. "We'd be flying right into the storm." But perhaps he could fly a more southerly route, ride the Nevada-California line. "We're only twenty minutes or so flying time out of Reno. I can put down there until the weather breaks. Then we'd just have a quick hop over the Sierra Nevadas to San Francisco."

He began the slow turn that would put him on a southern course. "Go sit down and buckle up," he told Rebecca.

Before he could complete the turn, the plane started to vibrate. Rebecca lost her balance and was thrown to the steel deck. The children sent up a collective squeal.

The plane felt like it was shaking itself to pieces.

Rebecca dragged herself up, her elbow feeling as if it'd been stung by a hundred wasps. The pain made her eyes water. With a heart-thumping feeling of menace and dread, she clung to the copilot's seat. "What's happened?"

Parnell's hands flew over the control panel, then he held the wheel until his knuckles turned white. The way the plane handled confirmed his worst fear. "One of the engines threw a propeller," he said, his face stark. He feathered the engine and soon the vibration ceased. He tested the controls again. His heart sank. The ailerons and rudder wouldn't respond. The plane was losing altitude at a rapid rate. "I think the damn thing has cartwheeled through a wing, maybe even sheared off part of the tail."

Rebecca swallowed back the panic that threatened to overwhelm her. "What does that mean?"

"It means we're losing airspeed, altitude."

"But . . . you can make it to an airfield? Somewhere?" Her tone begged him to say yes.

With the loss of the rudder and ailerons Parnell could go up or down, but he couldn't complete the turn and bank. The more altitude he reached the worse the weather, and in any case the weight of the ice was pushing them down. Even now he could feel the remaining propellers clawing at the rarified air. The best he could hope for was a glide path that didn't end in the face of a mountain. He muttered an epithet. "I'm going to have to set her down," he said.

Dread mushroomed inside Rebecca. "In the Rockies?" She could barely form the words.

"The Sierra Nevadas," he said grimly and turned all his concentration to keeping the plane level. He put on the radio headset, calling up Reno. Static hurt his ears, but he kept talking, giving his position, his glide path. If Reno was listening, static drowned them out. He tried Boise control, then Sacramento. But he was out of Boise airspace, Sacramento didn't respond. Parnell glanced at his altimeter. They were too low on the eastern slope of the Sierras. Sacramento didn't even know they existed.

For a moment Rebecca was mesmerized by the amalgam of green lighted dials, the pinpoints of red light. She jerked her gaze away from the instrument panel. "Can we dump some of the cargo? Can—"

Parnell shook his head. "You've been watching too many movies. Open a cargo door and we'd all be sucked out."

"Can you call somebody?"

Parnell almost laughed. "Sure, 911 to the rescue." They were already in the dead zone, at an altitude that wiped them off any radar that might have been tracking them.

"Damn you! We're going to die and you're being cute!" Rebecca gasped. As if in a nightmare her entire body felt leaden and immovable.

Parnell looked into her face. "Do you feel like your number is up?"

Rebecca was numb. "We're going to crash into the side of a mountain."

"I don't feel like my number's been called. I've been up against it before. You just got to have faith."

"In you?" she choked.

He gave her a thin smile. "I'm afraid I'm your best hope. Now go back there and quiet those kids, check seat belts and strap yourself in. Heads down." He gave her a sudden look of compassion. "Just leave the driving to me."

He knew he couldn't stop their descent. If a mountain didn't stop them, they had a chance.

Rebecca wanted to take each of the children in her arms, hold them, croon to them. Oh, to end their lives like this, she thought miserably. Pride. That's why she was on this plane. Trying to outsmart Parnell Stillman. Her pride was going to kill her, the children. And they'd never even had a chance to live. She forced a rising panic out of her voice. "We're going to have to land," she said. "It may be bumpy, so we have to put our heads down."

"Are we going to die?" Jonesy asked.

"Nobody'll miss us if we do," added Santee.

"We're not going to die! Put your heads down or I'm going to switch some behinds." It was an idle threat, but the children complied.

No one cried now. They were too frightened. They just waited.

Parnell worked the controls. After one minute, two, the plane leveled out, the three remaining engines strained to keep the heavy plane airborne. He marked a glide path and held the wheel. The plane shot out of the overcast. The altimeter dipped below the ten-thousand-foot mark. He flicked on the landing lights and strained his eyes through the windshield.

Rebecca and the children sat frozen, tensed for the inevitable crash. Above the ragged whine of the engines, Rebecca could hear Parnell talking to the plane, as if it were a woman, sweet-talking to get what he wanted of her. At one point he sighed like a satisfied lover.

Out the window Rebecca could make out trees poking through the snow covering the mountains. As the plane dropped lower, she could make out the jagged summits rising above the wing tips. Her mouth went dry. She prayed. She could hear herself murmuring assurances to the children. She ached for them. Too young! Please God, spare them. A belly-hollowing fear overwhelmed her, took away her ability to think or speak.

"Hallelujah!" Parnell breathed. He found what he'd been looking for as he'd jockeyed the plane through a valley; a flat, snow-covered meadow. It was going to be a do-or-die approach and he knew it. Landing gear up. No time for the formality of a checklist run-through, no time to reassure Rebecca Hollis or the children. He yelled for them to keep their heads down.

The sea of trees disappeared beneath the nose of the cockpit. Relying greatly on his depth perception, Parnell cut off the ignition and stalled the plane a scant fifteen feet above the ground. The plane fell, its underside hit the snow—a belly whop that jarred teeth and bones—it bounced, then took to the snow like a ski, yawing and pitching, picking up speed as if the meadow were a giant slalom course and the best time to beat was Time itself.

The nose cone plowed into the snow, spewing it out of its path, into the slowing propellers, onto the wings until the whole of the plane became one giant snow-plow. The meadow rose into the treeline. Parnell blanched, threw his arms up to protect his face. He had never decided whether he was Episcopalian or Presbyterian. He covered himself, decided he was both. He prayed his passengers survived, hoped God was noticing his last prayer was for others, unselfish. The nose cone lifted on the incline of the meadow's end, the plane slewed, fishtailing, pointed itself at the forest. Then it came awkwardly to a stop, shuddered and slowly slid back down the incline. Parnell lowered his arms.

A sudden deep silence engulfed the plane.

Santee was the first to react. He let out his breath. It sounded loud in the silence.

Parnell turned slowly and stared at Rebecca, ashen-faced. His voice cracked. "We made it."

"Thank God," she said.

Molly threw up.

3

"ARE WE DEAD?" whispered Nicholas. His unseeing eyes were wide, his hands going up to touch his nose, his ears, his neck.

Rebecca discovered that tears were coursing down her cheeks. She swiped at them. "No. No, we aren't." Thank you, Heavenly Father. Her elbow ached fiercely. She savored the pain. It meant she was truly alive.

Santee remained rigid, but stoically he was sitting up, as were Jonesy and Yancy. Molly had stopped retching.

"Anyone hurt?" Parnell asked.

Rebecca's eyes eyes met his. "I don't think so."

Parnell had regained about half of his composure, about eighty percent of his legs were back under him. All of his senses went into emergency mode. He sniffed for smoke, the smell of aviation fuel. The snow must've acted as a retardant, he thought, else they'd have already burst into flames.

Rebecca wanted to ask, "What now?" but she didn't. Somehow it seemed enough for the moment that they had all survived the harrowing drop from the air. She got out of her seat, teetered to a standing position. Had Molly not urgently needed looking after she would've sat back down.

It was dim and shadowy inside the plane. Except for the cockpit, most of the windows were blocked by the snow the plane had displaced as it made its terrifying slide. Rebecca coaxed Molly to her feet and down the tilting aisle to the rear of the plane. The cargo had shifted, they wove in and out of mail carts to get to the lavatory. No water came out of the pressurized faucet, she used paper towels.

"We almost saw God, didn't we?" said Molly.

"Almost," Rebecca replied, amazed that her voice sounded so normal.

"I wish we had, I want to talk to Him."

"He hears your prayers."

"No, He don't," Molly said with the utter conviction of a five-year-old who determines all in black and white and nothing in between.

Excitement had activated the children's kidney's, one by one they trooped to the rear of the plane. Rebecca gathered up their scattered totes into a pile and sat down. Parnell was struggling with the door.

"Can I help?" she asked.

"It's coming." He was met by a wall of packed snow. Rebecca breathed deeply and shivered from the sudden chill that permeated the cabin. Parnell went to a box anchored to the cabin wall. From it he took a hatchet and shovel, the kind that folds neatly into itself. He snapped it open and attacked the snow. It took ten minutes for him to hack out a hole large enough to squirm through.

"Damnation!" he groaned. Going headfirst was a mistake. The outer edge of snow was soft and he tumbled fifteen feet down snow banked against the plane.

He clawed his way up again, made his way onto the wing and gaped at the wake the plane had created the length of the meadow. In some places the meadow shimmered darkly where the heavy plane had skimmed down to frozen earth.

A vibration suddenly shook the plane followed by a sharp cracking noise. Parnell was thrown off balance. He lay flat on the ice-encrusted wing, then raised his head. The ground beneath the damaged fuselage was shaking, opening! He couldn't make his brain believe what his eyes were seeing. The hole in the ground enlarged, began to slowly swallow up the tail. Parnell clawed his way back inside the plane.

"Out! Everyone!" he shouted.

"But—" Rebecca began.

Jonesy came out of the bathroom. "That toilet flushes up," he said. The deck tilted and he tumbled backward.

"We've landed on a frozen lake. The ice is breaking up. The plane's sinking!"

Rebecca was nearest Parnell. He yanked her and shoved her out the door.

"The children!" she screamed as she fell down the snowdrift.

Parnell pushed them out so fast one tumbled atop the other into a heap. Jonesy was the last to come flailing down.

"Move!" Parnell yelled as he dove out the plane. He gained his feet and grabbed the nearest youngster. "The treeline," he huffed. They made it to the safety of solid ground and huddled together while their legs twitched and trembled.

Parnell counted heads. Satisfied there were no stragglers, he turned and watched gloomily as the tail and fuselage of his plane sank beneath the cold black water. The water sloshed up to the hole he'd hacked in the snow and began to pour into the cabin. He couldn't understand it. God had let him live only to allow nature to thwart him. He waited for the entire plane to disappear into the black hole. It didn't. But three quarters of it was submerged. The nose cone jutted up looking like the snout of a silvery shark, held there by an air pocket or submerged ice.

"That's the end of Stillman's," he said morosely. When he got back to Boise he'd have to tolerate one investigation and inspection after another to qualify for government contracts again. It might take years. He gave Rebecca a dark look. She was bad luck, a jinx. If he hadn't allowed her and those mini-monsters on his plane he'd be landing in San Francisco right about now.

"Is that all you can think of? Yourself?" Rebecca asked, torn between anger and the lingering relief of having survived more danger than she'd ever faced in her life.

"Don't speak to me," Parnell growled.

Rebecca's eyes blazed. "I will speak to you. We're in this together whether you like it or not. Now, how long before we're rescued, do you think? What are we supposed to do? We can't just stand here, we'll freeze."

"There's an ELT, an emergency locator transmitter in the tail. It trips in the event of a crash. Signals are picked up by SARSAT, the Search and Rescue Satellite-Aided Tracking system."

"You mean it's like a radio beam that says where we are?"

"Something like that. *If* the batteries are working, *if* it transmits underwater, *if* the signal is strong enough."

Parnell didn't mention that ninety-seven percent of ELT signals were false alarms. ELTs were never ignored, but it might take time to run down which plane, from what airport, might be missing. If the ELT was working, a ground crew could take a precise bearing from sixty miles away—under ideal conditions. Unfortunately nothing about their situation was ideal, not the weather nor the fact that most of the plane was under water and ice. And even under the best conditions, it would take days to coordinate rescue efforts. He scrutinized the formidable chunk of rough terrain that surrounded them on all sides. At least days, he thought grimly. A glance at Rebecca's face warned him not to mention that, either.

It was taking Rebecca a few seconds to register his words. Blood drained from her face. "You mean nobody knows where we are?"

"Not precisely. I guess we're about a hundred or two land miles off course. But somebody will," he added laconically. "Eventually."

"Do *you* know where we are?"

Glumly, Parnell hunched deeper into his sheepskin coat. "Roughly. I could plot it within a few degrees." They were probably forty miles from civilization in any direction, he thought. Which in this desolate wilderness might as well be a thousand. He looked up at the sky. The opening he'd found in the overcast had closed. It was cold. And was going to get colder. "We'll stay near the plane," he said. "On the off-chance Reno control locked in where we went off radar."

Yancy wiped his runny nose on his sleeve. "Don't do that," Rebecca chastised, rummaging for a tissue in a pocket and handing it to him.

"This is good country," announced Santee.

"Stay where I can see you," Rebecca warned him. To Parnell she said, "We at least need a fire."

Leave it to a woman to state the obvious, Parnell thought. "Right. Do you have any matches?"

"No, do you?"

Parnell sagged. It sure as hell wasn't his day. He knew he was going to have to get back inside the plane, retrieve his charts, maps, flares, dye, survival kit, and anything else that might be of use. Muttering a string of expletives he stared dourly at the open stretch of water between the shore and the plane.

"Please don't use that kind of language around the children," Rebecca said.

"Well, geez! Pardon me." He looked down his nose at her. "You got any better words that fit our predicament?" The thin-skinned goody-goody, he thought, and was reminded more than ever why he didn't like women. What grievous error in life had he ever committed to earn himself this kind of punishment? Stuck out in the wilderness with a woman and a bunch of kids who needed mollycoddling! He believed in God, didn't he? He paid his taxes, didn't he? Hell, he even put on a tie and went to church on Christmas. He didn't deserve this kind of misery. He shrugged deeper into his jacket.

"I'll tell you something, Miss Hollis. Don't goad me. If I was by myself I'd already be hightailing it out of here. If I hadn't had to worry with your safety, I'd've had time to grab my kit and maps."

Rebecca put her arms protectively about Molly and Nicholas. "A comment like that doesn't deserve a response. If it's any consolation to you, I can't imagine what I've ever done to end up plane-wrecked with the likes of you."

"Yes, well, you could be worse off."

"I don't see how."

"We could be dead," offered Jonesy.

The truth of that could not be contested. "Button your jacket," Rebecca told him sharply.

Jonesy shared a glance with the other children. Who understood grown-ups? it signaled.

Rebecca slipped inside herself, wondering how she was going to cope. She'd suffered emotional and financial setbacks in her life, but those paled in comparison to what she now faced. Every icy breath was torture to her lungs. Menace seemed to breathe through the whole vast stillness of the forest that rose at their backs. The long and short of it was their very lives now depended upon an obnoxious, disagreeable, self-centered bully.

Parnell had turned his attention to the lake, anticipating his dunking in the frigid water. He was having to dig deep inside himself to muster all his inner fortitude. Shoot! He didn't even like taking cold showers in ninety-degree heat. At the edge of his awareness he sensed Rebecca's eyes tracking him. She was looking at him as if she'd been eavesdroping on his thoughts. Which she probably was. With a woman you could never tell where danger lurked.

"What're you staring at?" he asked, scowling.

"Nothing! I was just wishing you'd been able to get the plane all the way onto solid ground."

"Would the face of a mountain have been solid enough for you?"

"I wish you'd quit taking everything I say the wrong way."

"I take it like I hear it."

"Well, hear this: don't you think you should quit taking potshots at me and figure out how we're going to get out of this mess?"

Parnell clicked his heels together and gave her a parade-ground salute. "Why, most assuredly, ma'am. At once, ma'am. You just leave every little old detail to me. Why, I'll just jump through that hoop you're rolling, like the cavalry to the rescue." He relaxed his stance and shoved his hands into his pockets. "What do you think this is? A John Wayne movie?"

Rebecca restrained a sudden urge to slap him. "I won't be put off by a display of silly sarcasm. You're the one who put us down in this . . . this wilderness. Now, if you don't have any suggestions, at least point us in the right direction. We'll walk out of here by ourselves."

"That's the stupidest thing I've ever heard. Look at the sky. Those clouds are fixing to dump snow like you've never seen. You and those kids would get maybe a mile. You'd freeze to death. What do you know about survival?"

"Enough to know that we can't just stand here and argue."

"True enough," he relented, facing once again his own truth in the matter: the icy water between the shore and the plane. He'd have to try it. He was probably going to die. He'd be lauded a martyr, a hero even, if any one of his passengers got out alive to tell the story. He'd be admired for his skill in getting the plane down without running into the face of mountain, too. He would be awarded a tiny, but indelible place in aviation history.

Posthumously.

However, if God decided to take him into His fold he didn't want an audience of children. He called to the boy who appeared the oldest, least scared and most alert. "What's your name?"

"Santee."

"You're the one with Indian in him, right?"

"One-quarter Sioux," Santee said, his dark eyes shuttered.

"Good. It's time to make your ancestors proud of you. See that tree? Using it as your center I want you to count off loud and clear a hundred paces in the snow. Turn around and follow your own tracks back, then do it again, like making spokes in a wheel. You get about a dozen spokes, you tramp along the outside of 'em forming a circle. Then you put everybody to work finding wood, logs and so on, for a fire. Drag it back to the middle of the circle. And, nobody goes outside the circle. Got that?"

All eyes were on Parnell. He felt the weight of them.

"I got it," Santee said.

Rebecca protested. "They might get lost in the forest!"

He sighed. "I just told them how not to."

"I'm responsible for them."

"There can only be one person in charge—me." Unless I'm dead, he thought.

"I'm better able to deal with the children."

"You want to be in charge?" Parnell fixed her with a malicious glare. "I'll tell you where the matches are and you go get them."

"I'll be more than happy to," Rebecca replied in kind.

Parnell pointed to the submerged plane.

"But . . ." Rebecca slumped against the cold bark of a tree. "There's no way to get aboard."

"Yes, there is. Swim."

Her hands went limp at her sides. "I couldn't. I don't know how."

"I guess that decides the issue on all fronts, doesn't it?" Parnell waved to Santee. "Get on with it." The children lined up single file. Nicholas brought up the rear, his hand on Molly's shoulder for guidance. They tramped off, making a game of it.

"I'll go with them," Rebecca said.

Parnell grabbed her arm. She yelped.

He jerked his hand back. "You hurt?"

"I hit my funny bone."

Parnell took her measure. It was good that she didn't complain about every little bump and bruise. But still, in his book it was too late to allow himself to be friendly. "I'll check it later." He told her what he expected to retrieve from the plane. Told her what to do if he didn't make it.

Rebecca blanched. "Please, don't attempt it if you think you can't make it." The idea of suddenly being alone with only the children, the idea of not having a man to take charge, to save them, caused her rib cage to contract painfully.

The winter-gray clouds were lowering. Parnell looked from the sky to Rebecca. In an offhand way, her concern made him feel good. Except for Uncle Henry, nobody in the world had ever cared whether he lived or died.

"If it goes against me, just remember that in a week, maybe less, the lake will refreeze. Then you can just walk out to the plane."

"A week?" Her voice was almost nonexistent. "How would we survive a week?"

His smile was a grim expression of forbearance. "Well, that's the problem, isn't it?"

The wind was picking up. Rebecca turned her collar up and held it closed. Snow devils swirled, disappeared into the rippling surface surrounding the plane. "What do you want me to do?"

"Follow orders."

"I'll try."

"All you have to do for the moment is spot me. And if . . . well, you be sure to tell old Amos I said—" Parnell embarrassed himself by almost choking up. "Ah, hell!"

Rebecca swallowed on a dry throat. She realized instinctively that she could not afford to let reality beat her down. Death as a possibility she couldn't consider, not the pilot's, hers, or the children's. She had to cling mindlessly to the idea that rescue was not beyond hope. She had to be practical. "Can you get our totes, you think? My suitcase?"

"You want a change of clothes and lipstick?" Parnell bellowed. "What's it going to take to make you understand the seriousness of our situation!"

"There're some sandwiches in one of the totes. And the thermos."

"All right." He forced his tone to a normal level. "I'll try to find them." He moved to the edge of the lake. Rebecca followed.

In the distance they could hear the children's voices, led by Santee. "Twelve, ho! Thirteen, ho!"

Parnell began to unlace his boots. He stripped down to his long underwear, handing each piece of clothing to Rebecca as he disrobed. Then he hesitated. His toes were already turning blue. Goose bumps covered his flesh. If he made it back, he'd need the insulating qualities of his long johns. "Turn your head," he said to Rebecca.

"You aren't . . . ?"

"I have to." He looked at the deadly water. He hoped the lake was truly that and not some wide stretch of river or stream boasting strong currents that would drag him from the open water and thrust him beneath the ice. Rebecca closed her eyes and held out her hand to receive his underwear.

Like all pilots, most of whom were closet romantics, Parnell had daydreamed of himself in the role of rescuer. Now that the opportunity was thrust upon him, he wished he could take back every one of those dreams. He put a toe tentatively into the frigid water. The shock of it shot up into his chest and made his heart skip. But it was too late now to weigh his chances of success. "I hope my pecker doesn't freeze off," he said dolefully. Then with bravado summoned strictly for Rebecca's benefit, he cast his naked, goose-bump-crawling body full tilt into the lake.

The scream in his throat was seized up by the icy water.

Rebecca had a glimpse of wide shoulders, knobby backbone, tapered waist; registered, too, that his lean posterior was somewhat lighter than the skin on his back, a telling reminder of a once-bronze summer tan. She kept her eyes riveted on him, praying desperately that he'd make it. He was kicking his feet, sending up geysers of water, flailing the surface with his arms. He can't swim, either, she thought, yet he was making progress and she realized that his actions were probably designed to distract him from the freezing water and to keep his blood circulating. She felt impotent, standing there, just watching.

She draped his coat over her shoulders, glad of the extra warmth, then feeling guilty that she was warm and he wasn't, she opened her coat and pressed the rest of his clothes to her body. It'd help some when he donned them again, she thought. It wasn't much, but it was the best she could do. As the cold went out of his sweater, the faint man smell of soap and oil clung to her.

Parnell's head bobbed, his arms seemed to be tiring. He went under the water. Rebecca held her breath and when Parnell didn't reappear she let it out in a scream.

There was a sudden silence at her back, the children had left off chanting. They straggled out of the trees and joined her on the shore. The frightened look on Rebecca's face stifled their questions.

Parnell's head suddenly surfaced, they could hear his sputtering, his gasping. Impulsively, the children applauded, yelled. For one brief moment the captain turned in their direction. Then he hooked his hand over one of the flaps and moved along the wing until he was at the body of the plane. Water flowing over the threshold and into the cabin when the fuselage sunk had knocked away the snow. Ice was forming on every surface. It took him two tries to lift himself into the cabin.

Rebecca could imagine what strength it must have cost him, for he no more gained his feet, silhouetted in the door, than his naked body seemed to shiver uncontrollably. He stumbled out of their sight.

"What's happening?" Nicholas pleaded.

"Captain Stillman's got inside the plane."

"He took off all his clothes," said Molly. "He's blue."

Santee, counting himself in charge of the fire bri-gade, ordered the children back to work. "There're some fallen trees," he said to Rebecca. "We can scrape the bark off, to have it ready."

"That's good, Santee."

"You want me to stay with you instead?"

She shook her head. "I'll yell if I need you. Firewood is more important."

"We'll need a shelter, too."

Rebecca smiled. "You're thinking ahead, but one thing at a time." And because she needed reassurance, even if it came out of her own mouth, she added, "We'll wait for Captain Stillman to direct us on the best place to build it. I believe he wants us to stay near the plane."

Santee hurried to catch up with the others, walking, Rebecca thought, as if he knew right where life was leading him. She watched him join the others. Molly, in her heavy shoes and Yancy in her footsteps were straggling. But it was something for them to do. They were participating in an adventure. She envied them their activity. She turned back toward the plane, pac-ing up and down the shore to keep warm, her eyes locked on the door for a glimpse of the pilot.

PARNELL WAS STANDING in icy water, thigh-deep. He had tried to drag one of the mail carts uphill in the aisle, but it was so water-logged its weight was beyond his strength. He couldn't get to the locker where the raft, its pockets filled with rations, was stored. He was sucking breaths of cold air that made his teeth stab with pain. Think! he told himself. Grab what you can for now. The plane isn't going anywhere. Matches. Don't forget matches. Totes. Suitcase.

The carts had wooden lids. He hacked one loose with the hatchet. He sloshed through the water and carried it back to the door. He loaded it up, then discovered the folly of that. He couldn't shove it out of the plane without tilting it and everything sliding off. Not thinking straight, he thought. His brain was responding sluggishly.

He made himself stop, plan.

Pile everything by the door. Put the makeshift raft in the water first and load it while he kept it balanced with his feet. That would work. Then he'd push the raft off and lower himself into the water after it. Yes. That was better. He'd have more control.

For an instant his eyes fastened on Rebecca as she paced the shore. Not a mirage, he thought, not a bad dream. He blinked. Faintly, he could hear the high-voiced chants of the kids. He hoped he could make it back to them. If not, maybe the raft would float toward shore where Rebecca could reach it. His teeth began to chatter uncontrollably.

THE COLD WAS NOW almost beyond his endurance, his toes so stiffened he couldn't curl them to grasp the decking. Painfully he made his way once more to the cockpit for his maps, his personal survival kit, anything else that might be useful.

He stubbed his toe, the pain was excruciating. He lifted the foot, lost his balance, fell and began to slide backward down the tilted aisle. The steel floor was roughly made, full of burrs, they cut into the flesh of his backside like hundreds of tiny sharp razors. The downward slide carried him into the sloshing water; he slammed into one of the submerged mailcarts. He yelped. Too late he realized the folly of that as the dark icy water filled his mouth and nose. He raised his head, coughed and sputtered, gasping for breath. He used the mail cart for a brace to push himself up the aisle until his head was above the water.

He lay there limp and knew he was freezing. He could just stop here, he thought. They'd find his body. Naked. He didn't like the idea of that. Too undignified. Dying naked in bed was one thing, but elsewhere, a man ought to have his boots on. Or at least his pants.

He thought about Rebecca. When the lake froze she'd walk in and find him. The sight would probably make her go round the bend. He'd be blamed for that, too.

He forced an arm behind his head, felt for the leg of the row of seats, closed his fingers around it and began to pull himself up until he was entirely out of the water. Then, on his hands and knees, he crawled back to the cockpit.

He lay on his stomach to load the raft, then gently pushed it away lest his own drop back into the frigid waters topple it. He gathered his energy, braced his feet against the plane and pushed off.

He gasped, gagged, ground his teeth until his jaws ached but he managed to push the raft ahead of him. His course was erratic. And then he felt the soft thump as the wood slab scraped the shore.

He had made it! A sense of physical release surged through him. He slid back under the water.

Rebecca almost cried with relief when the pilot came back into view. His absence had seemed endless to her. But then his head and shoulders were framed in the opening and she'd watched him loading the raft. After he'd slid into the water he was again lost to her sight behind the loaded makeshift raft. She watched the board bobble, bump ice and slowly come towards her.

When it hit shore, she expected the pilot to rise up. He didn't. Beyond the raft she saw his head slip beneath the surface. She splashed into the shallows, felt the shock of the water as it poured in over the tops of her boots. How could he have borne this cold! Twice! Her stock in him went up. She grabbed him by his hair and backed up, dragging the limp weight of him until he was stretched out in the snow.

4

REBECCA'S THROAT CLAMPED DOWN to hold back a wail of hysteria. She didn't know what to do first. The pilot lay in the snow at her feet, his skin an unhealthy color. Yet even in the extremity of the moment she could not help but glance down at the wide plain of his chest, the concave of his belly and the dark hair at the juncture of his thighs. His was a good body. A body that a woman... She caught the drift of her musing and stopped in mid-thought. Her feet were so cold and wet she could hardly think straight!

The man needed immediate attention. But the raft was floating off! She covered him with his own coat then raced again into the water and pushed the raft until it was lodged firmly in the slush.

The children had gathered round Parnell. Their faces, flushed from exertion, wore stunned expressions.

"He's dead," said Yancy.

"No, he isn't!" Rebecca's voice sounded strained and unnatural to her; her heartbeat seemed to be forcing all the air out of her lungs. She wouldn't let him die. And if he did, she'd resurrect him. She had to. How else were they to live? She couldn't manage on her own. "Santee," she rasped, "unload that board. Find the survival kit, the matches. Can you build the fire?" She had no idea how long before they'd be rescued. "Be careful with the matches."

She bent over Parnell. His pulse felt weak. His eyelids twitched, there were no obstructions in his windpipe as far as she could tell, and he was breathing. She placed her hand on his chest, felt it rise and fall. She pressed her ear to his heart. It sounded strong. So what was the matter with him? Suffering from shock? Exposure? Hypothermia? It didn't matter. In any case, he needed warmth. She knelt down beside him. It was then she noticed the snow around him turning a deep red.

"I think he's bleeding," said Jonesy.

Fighting down her panic, Rebecca made a quick inspection. With Jonesy's help she turned the pilot over.

"Ooooo," Molly exclaimed.

For a moment Rebecca couldn't think, she was cold and numb. The pilot's lower back and rear were shredded and raw, oozing blood. She pushed Molly out of the way. "Go help Santee."

She got her own coat under Parnell. Kneeling in the snow she tried to dress him. It was like trying to drape clothes on a dead bear. The body that had seemed all loose bones was now too long of arm and leg, too broad of chest and had feet that defied even a pair of socks. Then she realized it was her own trembling hands that were defeating her. She instead wrapped him in his clothes, first the longjohns, then his shirt, sweater, his pants. She managed to get his socks on, but still his long legs were bare, thrusting out of the cocoon of clothing. She tore into her suitcase, found her flannel nightgown and wrapped his legs in that. "Oh, for a blanket," she moaned.

"I found the matches!" Santee shouted, holding up a waterproof tin.

"Thank God," Rebecca breathed. She lifted one of Parnell's hands and placed it in Nicholas's. "Rub his hands, Nicholas. Jonesy, you and Yancy each take a foot. Don't stop. It's important you keep his blood circulating. I'll help Santee get the fire going."

"I don't want to do anything, I'm tired," said Molly.

"I know you are sweetheart. We all are. But you'll have to do your share. You rub the captain's other hand. I've got to help Santee, and then we'll have a nice warm fire to cozy up to."

"When are we gonna eat?" called in Jonesy. "I've worked up an appetite."

Food. Hunger. Rebecca saw all of them starving, dwindling to skin and bones. Frozen to death in grotesque shapes. There were only a few of the egg sandwiches left, a six-pack of juice and the odd one from another pack, because she'd had coffee instead. She quickly went through the totes that were now scattered in the snow. She found the blue one that held the food and slipped the strap over her shoulder. "Once we have the fire going and the captain settled, we'll eat."

Our last meal until we're found, she thought.

It was a pitifully small heap of wood that the children had gathered.

"There's a big fallen tree we could make camp under," Santee said.

"Under?" Rebecca puzzled.

"It didn't fall all the way down. It's caught in the crook of another tree. We could use it as a lodgepole to lean branches against."

"Show me," Rebecca said. To her eyes it didn't look promising, but Santee was full of enthusiasm.

"We could build the fire here," he said pointing to a depression in the snow. "And I can chop limbs off the firs with the hatchet to make the sides of the shelter."

"First the fire," Rebecca said. She felt the stealthy invasion of the cold through her wet boots. If she suffered frostbite, she knew that she was doomed, the children along with her, notwithstanding Santee's knowledge of the forest. Suffering such discomfort made her estimation of the pilot go up. That he had had the courage, the wherewithal to brave the frigid water, to withstand . . . She wanted urgently to return to his side, check on him, see if he had yet regained consciousness.

A snowflake landed on her face. Rebecca looked up through the trees at the muted gray and dreary light, the low-sagging gray clouds. The true horror of their situation came over her again, filling her with an urgency unlike any she'd ever known.

The fire didn't come easy. She and Santee scraped away snow down to the frozen earth. He drew from his pocket scraps of dry twigs interwoven with down and feathers. "And old bird's nest," he said proudly. "It's dry."

Rebecca managed a smile. She knew his Indian folklore came mostly from books for he'd never lived on a reservation; his forestry skill came from one summer that he'd been with a family that had enrolled him in Boy Scouts. His dream was to be adopted by someone who loved the outdoors as much as he.

It took four matches, persistence and long agonizing minutes before a wisp of smoke rose from the ball of kindling. Santee blew it into a tiny flame. He fed it with bark chips and finally, a branch impregnated with damp. "Don't worry, it'll catch," he said. After a moment, it did. Rebecca exhaled a tension-filled sigh.

With careful placement Santee began to build the fire with somewhat larger pieces of wood. "You have to keep it stacked so there'll be a draw," he explained.

Snow around the edges of the depression began to melt. It trickled into the fire, made it hiss. Rebecca's heart lurched. She and Santee worked frantically to push back the snow with their bare hands. They managed to expose a ragged four-foot circle of earth. The flames leaped higher, the wood burning above the ground.

"I think it's okay for now," Rebecca said. She knelt a moment longer and put her palms toward the flames.

Fire was a human need so basic, so taken for granted in her life. She had never realized that lack of its comfort could be such a deprivation. Her mind flashed to a recent newscast about street people, about their plight in winter-whipped cities; scenes of men and women wrapping themselves in newspapers and sleeping in cardboard boxes. Bless them all, she thought.

She realized how rich in life, how privileged she'd been. So what, if she had not been well loved? Had had a miserable youth, an unhappy marriage? Her thoughts had often turned inward, she had revelled in self-pity. Never again, she thought.

Her feet began to ache, the pain a reminder that she was alive. She meant to stay that way. She'd be strong for all of them. She looked about for a branch from which to hang the food tote. She knew little about camping, but she recalled that on a school field trip all their lunches had been put in a box and stored in the crook of a tree against small and curious animals. Ants had gotten to them, but she supposed ants hibernated in winter. Like bears. Bears. Wolves. Stop it! she told herself. It was stupid to be inventing dangers when there were real ones yet to be dealt with.

Leaving Santee to tend the fire she went out of the forest and down the hill to the lake. Molly was sitting on the suitcase, her thumb in her mouth. Yancy sat next to her, crooning to his friend Scrappy. The pilot was folded into the fetal position.

"He started shivering and curled up," Jonesy said. "We couldn't stretch him back out."

"He said he wanted to sleep," informed Nicholas.

"He talked?"

"I just told you."

Rebecca kneeled down and shook Parnell, calling to him softly.

"Leave me," he groaned. "Save yourself."

"We're all saved," Rebecca said. "We have a fire built. Can you walk?"

Parnell's lids blinked open. Rebecca could see him struggling to focus, to drag himself from some deep lethargy. "Walk?" his voice cracked. "Can't walk out..."

"Just up the hill," she encouraged, putting an arm under his shoulders and tugging him into a sitting position. The weight of his body shifted to his backside. The howl came from far back in his throat. Rebecca was certain that he'd uttered a vulgar epithet, but it had come out garbled, and anyway, now was not the time to chastise him. Pain seemed to make him more alert. Perhaps he could help dress himself. To the children she said, "Each of you grab a tote. Jonesy, maybe you could handle the suitcase? Go on up to the fire, the captain and I will be along in a few minutes."

The falling snow was beginning to thicken. The wind was colder, stronger, whipping down the valley and across the frozen lake. Rebecca looked longingly at the plane. If only they'd been able to use it as shelter! On every side of the lake the forest stretched away in sweeping upward curves; up, up until peaks disappeared into a sodden gray. It seemed to Rebecca to be the picture of desolation. No bird fluttered, no animal moved. And yet, on a Christmas card it would be a winter scene, a thing of beauty. But it wasn't a mere scene. It was a harsh and uncompromising landscape. She felt small, a helpless speck of human matter. Her throat was dry. She realized she was thirsty. She turned to Parnell and began to unwrap the cocoon of clothing.

"Hey!" he protested, brushing weakly at her hands.

"I couldn't get your clothes on you before. You'll have to help me."

Parnell attempted to maintain a modicum of modesty, but he couldn't stand alone to step into his longjohns and pants. His hands shook as if palsied and he had to suffer the mortification of Rebecca zipping up his pants.

"Oh, hell," he said despairingly.

Rebecca looked into his face and smiled. She'd had another glimpse of his buttocks. More than a single layer of skin had been torn away. She could never have done what he had done. He had put his life on the line for her, for them all. He could've stayed with the plane, inside it. "I've never met a man so brave as you," she said shyly.

Parnell's blue lips suddenly flushed with color, as did the flesh beneath his beard stubble. No one had ever thought him brave before, not even when he'd been in the navy. Flying, surviving, those were things every pilot had to do. If one got out of a tight spot, why, one was just lucky. Nobody thought it brave, except maybe one's mother. He'd had Uncle Henry for a mother. And the old coot never recognized fear, much less bravery. Few other emotions, either. "It was nothing," he mumbled.

"It was everything," she replied.

It took some tugging to get his boots on. He leaned heavily on Rebecca and every struggling, uphill step caused pain. He had to clench his teeth to keep from groaning. By the time they reached the welcome warmth of the small fire perspiration was beading on his forehead. He dropped down to his knees, then lay on his side, crooking an arm beneath his head. His eyes closed. "Truth is, I'm beat," he said.

"I'm getting hungrier and hungrier," said Jonesy.

"Me, too," came the chorus.

Santee had dragged up a log. Rebecca sank wearily onto it. There wasn't enough food to really ration, but she wanted to wait as long as possible before they ate what was left of their snacks. Better to be hungry during the day, sleep on a full stomach. Then tomorrow...no, she couldn't deal with tomorrow. Each minute had to be dealt with as it came. She picked up a pinch of snow, put it on her tongue.

"You aren't supposed to do that," Yancy warned. "Santee said so."

"It cools your inside temperature," Santee added.

"Well, we have a fire, so let's agree that we only quench our thirst with snow if we can stay warm." Her feet were stinging. Frostbite? And snow was finding its way through the thick overhead foliage. "Let's all of us change our socks. Then we have to put up a shelter—"

"We can make a fort!" exclaimed Nicholas who was big on warfare. At the orphanage he played often with a set of carved wooden soldiers, their painted surfaces faded into pale replicas by his fondling to discern every tiny feature.

"Let's eat first," Jonesy persisted.

"We'll eat after we've got a roof over our heads, not before," Rebecca said firmly.

Yancy was rummaging through his things. "Everything in my tote is sopping wet!"

They each had only one change of clothing, for the conference was to be only a single day—tomorrow. They were supposed to fly back to Boise on the Sunday morning return mail flight. But now . . .

Nicholas said, "I wonder if everybody thinks we're dead."

"Who would care?" came from Santee.

Privately Rebecca wondered the same thing. She had been little more than an inconvenience to her parents. Her former husband? He'd be thankful that there was no longer a reminder of his first and failed marriage. "I care! Abigail cares. I'm sure we've already been reported missing. We're going to get through this."

"I'm tired of getting through things," said Yancy. "So is Scrappy."

Molly took her thumb out of her mouth. "Is somebody going to come get us before it gets dark?"

"I don't know." Rebecca glanced at the pilot. It wasn't fair that he was leaving all this to her. She wished she too could sleep, blot it out of her mind. Wake up and find it all a nightmare. "Let's hope so, but we have to prepare against the possibility that we won't be rescued today. Probably tomorrow." She rummaged in the suitcase, gave Yancy her only other pair of socks. "Put these on." She rolled the log closer to the fire. "We'll dry out the others on this." She tried to shake Parnell from his stupor.

"In a minute," he muttered gruffly.

"You wanted to take charge," she said into his ear. "Wake up and do it!"

He nodded his head slightly, but refused to be roused. Bravery notwithstanding, Rebecca began to thoroughly dislike him again. He was like every other man in her life who'd meant something to her—her father, her brother, her husband. Each of them had looked to his own needs before deigning to consider her own. Even then she'd had to suffer their condescension, victimized by their male attitudes and her own feminity.

Her feet hurt, her elbow hurt, she had to build a shelter while the pilot got his beauty sleep. They were lost in the wilderness and she was scared! It wasn't fair. Life wasn't fair! She shook her head as if to jar the thoughts. She'd learned that about a thousand years ago hadn't she? Why so disappointed now? Because she felt so isolated, that was why. She wanted someone to care about her, to be upset that she was lost. She wanted a champion out there in the civilized world telling the authorities to find her!

She started guiltily. She was drowning in self-pity again.

It would be nice to be at the center of someone's life. There! That was better.

She looked down at the pilot. But not the center of his life, the skinny, selfish, thoughtless worm. As she turned away to help Molly with her clumsy shoes, a contradiction popped unwillingly into conscious thought. He wasn't all that skinny. If anything, he was ... No! She wouldn't get caught up in that kind of thinking. Not even if he was the last man on earth.

Then it came to her. The pilot might be the last adult man she'd ever see. For her, he might be the last man on earth. The idea of that caused renewed energy to surge through her. Be damned if I'll settle for the likes of him, she thought.

Still, she was ashamed of having tried to awaken him. He deserved a good sleep after what he done for them, after what he'd been through.

A sudden gust of wind soughed through the tree-tops. A shower of snow fell from the swaying branches. A chunk fell into the fire, hissing as it melted. "All right, Santee, let's get this show on the road. C'mon kids, we've got a shelter to construct."

It took two hours to locate enough of the evergreen firs small enough in diameter to attack with the small hatchet. Rebecca took turns with Santee lopping off branches on the sides of the young trees that would serve as "walls." The hacked-off branches were used as thatching. In a gully they discovered a bed of black crowberry shrubs and these they chopped for bedding to keep them off the frozen earth.

Molly had long since given up and stayed by the fire, as had Nicholas, for without a guide, he kept wandering into trees and falling down gullies. They were within several yards of camp when Rebecca heard Molly's wail.

"It's not my fault!" the child was keening over and over.

Rebecca dropped her load of branches and raced into camp.

Parnell was outside the meager green bower swaying on his feet, but seeming to lord it over Nicholas and Molly. "What's going on?" Rebecca shouted. "What have you done to them!"

Eyes watering, he whirled about on unsteady legs, waving a rough hand toward the shelter. Smoke was pouring out the opening, gray wisps trailing skyward. "They set the damned thing on fire."

"We didn't," snuffled Molly. Rebecca pushed that log up to the fire, to dry our socks on."

"I could've burned up!" Parnell said succinctly.

"I wish you had," Rebecca cried. "You've left us to— Oh!" She swiped at a tear with a dirty knuckle, the tears provoked as much by anger as fear and frustration. "Our socks burned up?"

Parnell was spoiling for a fight. The choking stinging smoke had awakened him from the best dream he'd had in years. He'd gone to sleep on the words that Rebecca had found him brave and he'd enjoyed seeing himself in the noble role of a champion, however meaningless and futile and unreal. From pleasant slumber he'd leaped confused to his feet, hit his head on the lodgepole, fallen to his knees and crawled in ten different directions before he'd found the way out. Now he was hurting so he wasn't sure if he was on the stony road of life or the path to hell. Did Rebecca Hollis care?

Hell, no! All she cared about was socks. He gave her a look of utter ill favor.

"We can manage without a pair of socks," he snarled. Her coat had spilled open, her sweater was unbuttoned, a gap in her blouse revealed a view of great aesthetic interest. Hah! He was a man who could rise above that trick. The tears, too.

"You can say that because yours are dry. Mine aren't."

"Well, have mine!" He plopped down and wished immediately that he hadn't. His backside felt on fire.

Rebecca saw the wince of pain move across the pilot's features. "Keep your old smelly socks on," she said.

The children exchanged cautious glances. Nicholas couldn't share their looks, but the discord between the adults affected his sensitive instincts. "I think we're in big trouble," he whispered behind his hand.

"I guess I'll just put out the fire before the whole thing goes up," said Santee, which brought the two adults back to sanity of a sorts.

"I'll help," said Rebecca.

"So will I," said Parnell, stiff of lip and body. "But we'll leave the fire going, rebuild the lean-to."

He directed them to dismantle one whole side of the lean-to.

Rebecca had longed for Parnell to give them some direction, but now that he was actually doing it, she considered him a villain usurping her authority. "All that work for nothing!" she snapped, eyeing him with one in her arsenal of deadly looks.

"If you're going to do something, you should do it right the first time," he replied loftily. "That's what my old Uncle Henry used to say. Bless his departed soul."

"We're not any one of us interested in Stillman family platitudes," said Rebecca, calling to the fore all the sarcasm she could muster.

Parnell stopped piling snow on the smoldering limbs. "You're ungrateful, you know that? I almost died for you." His fanny stung like crazy, a constant reminder of how unselfish he'd been. He threw it in. "I left some of the best skin I own out on that plane. What more do you want?"

"To be in San Francisco would be nice."

His lips curled down. She was still trampling on his sense of heroics. "I'll bet all your life you've been told you're unreasonable."

"I most assuredly have; mostly by overbearing despots who were forever trying to convince me that they were always right. Just like you're doing."

Parnell's stomach drew up into knots. He'd have bleeding ulcers before he got them back to civilization, not to mention his arse was probably scarred for life. "I'm right because I know more than you."

"You do not!"

"We'll see," he said, turning away to bark out orders to any of the kids who'd listen.

"Lift bale, tote barge, bully-bully," Rebecca said to his back. Her anger diminished when she glanced at her hands. All of her nails were broken. But not her spirit, she thought. In her life she'd survived far worse than broken nails and a grubby face. She'd survived a lifetime of Parnell Stillmans. This adventure—she wasn't going to name it a tragedy—was just going to make her stronger. Give her insights into herself that she hadn't had. She could hold her own. Above all, she wasn't going to allow fear or Parnell Stillman to rule her.

The lean-to was reconstructed with a small gap at the top to carry out the smoke. The brush collected for bedding was hauled inside. The wood gathered to feed the fire was stacked around the inside edges of the shelter.

Finally, with the storm swirling full force upon them, there was nothing left but to crawl inside and crouch by the fire.

IT WAS CROWDED AND DIM inside the shelter, the only light coming from flickering flames. Rebecca felt almost suffocated by the greenery and shrubbery. It was above her head, at her back and beneath her hips. Small limbs and knotty wood poked up through the cushiony brush to stab her derriere. She sat lotus fashion and stared with dismay at the meager supply of food and drink which she had spread out on the ground before her.

"Everything's frozen," she said forlornly.

Parnell went outside and brought in a small log, placing it strategically near the base of the fire.

"Line everything up on this. We'll watch it. This time."

Rebecca glanced up from her dismay. "Stop baiting me. Burning up the socks was an accident."

"So was losing my plane," he snapped, aggrieved.

He was envying Rebecca her ability to sit. He could not at the moment absorb the torment of sticks and twigs jabbing into his posterior. The children had taken the snug deep end of the shelter, which left him to arrange his lanky frame laterally near the opening, the coldest spot.

Rebecca felt she had aged ten years since that morning. Exhaustion and stress were taking its toll. She felt as limp and ragged as the pilot looked. Had she been certain of rescue within a few hours, even a day, she wouldn't back down. But a wreck in the wilderness was a far cry from a flat tire on the highway where help was as near as the first cruising highway patrol. Even with her limited knowledge, she knew the snowstorm would hinder search planes. They were locked together in a life-threatening situation at least until the storm abated. If they were to survive she and the pilot would have to come to terms, somehow.

"Don't you think we need to stop going for each other's throats? I know the crash was an accident. And ... and it was a brave thing you did—swimming out to the plane for matches and all."

"Well..." said Parnell, somewhat mollified, redeeming a speck of his battered ego.

"And truly," continued Rebecca placatingly, "I wouldn't have made any cracks at all if you hadn't been so obnoxious from the very first."

"You just had to say that, didn't you? You can't say one nice thing and leave it alone. You're persecuting me on purpose."

"You're the one! You badger and bully all of us. You can't expect me to just lie back and take it."

They argued another thirty minutes.

Arms hugging their legs and chins propped on knees, the children stared at the adults stolidly with expressionless faces and glazed eyes.

"When can we eat?" injected Jonesy in a small voice when Parnell paused to inhale, Rebecca to form a sharp riposte.

With a last look of umbrage, Rebecca turned from Parnell and attempted to pass out the sandwiches. His hand shot out and closed over her wrist.

"Not yet!"

Rebecca jerked loose. "Keep your hands off me."

A pocketknife materialized from his pocket and he thrust the point of it into the log. "Don't touch the food."

"I suppose you want it all for yourself. Survival of the fittest and all that."

In his indignation Parnell virtually gargled his words. "We have to satisfy our craving for food as well as our hunger. You put a piece on your tongue and hold it there for the count of ten. Then you chew." He cut the sandwiches into bite-sized pieces, dividing the portions into seven.

"Chew egg?"

"Chew! Like this." He demonstrated, exaggerating the movement of his jaw. The kids laughed. "It's not funny." He glowered until they produced solemn expressions. "Chew twenty times before you swallow."

"He's right," said Santee. "It makes the food last longer, makes it satisfying. That's what it said in one of my books."

Parnell beamed at him in approval.

"I can't hold it in my mouth," Jonesy said around the morsel of bread. "I have to swallow."

Parnell reached over and clamped the boy under his jaw. "Count! Now chew . . . now swallow!"

Jonesy began to sniffle.

"Did you have to do that?" Rebecca yelled. "Can't you be kind? These children have all been hurt at the hands of adults. They're orphans!"

Parnell moved to sit on his buttocks and grimaced. He couldn't seem to come out ahead lying on his side, with his head propped in the palm of his hand. "They can either be dead orphans or live orphans. You pick. And another thing, stop shoving that down my throat. Just because a person is an orphan doesn't mean he gets the world on a string to dawdle with. Or goes around making people feel sorry for him. An orphan's gotta learn to handle it. I know—from experience."

Firelight flickered, casting shadows across Rebecca's delicate, albeit dirty, features. "You were an orphan?"

"Damned right! And I turned out just fine."

"I see." Her voice was carefully leached of expression. She reasoned that disputing his idea of how he had turned out would carry them far into the night.

"Common sense, that's all we need," Parnell said. "Not bellyaching."

Rebecca nodded and picked up a tidbit of sandwich. She held it on her tongue to the count of ten, then chewed. It tasted as good as anything she'd ever eaten in her life.

5

AT DUSK, or what Rebecca supposed was the hour of dusk—her watch had stopped after plunging her arm underwater to grasp the pilot—the sky seemed to open, dumping great swirling drifts of snow. Outside the shelter the dark became oppressive, the snow appearing not white but purple. She estimated that they had been plane-wrecked for eleven or twelve hours. It already felt like days.

Inside the shelter each of them had a space near the fire, taking warmth from it and from each other. But it wasn't at all like sitting in the parlor after supper at the orphanage. There was no Abigail to chat with, no television to watch, no book to read, no toy to occupy an hour. Conversation was mostly among the children. Listening to their low excited voices, she could tell they found their situation to be high adventure.

The surge of adrenaline that had kept her going was draining away. She felt wobbly, fatigued. She wanted to sleep, but didn't dare close her eyes until the children fell soundly asleep. As yet, not one of them seemed inclined to do so.

"I have to go to the bathroom," said Molly.

"So do I," said Nicholas.

Parnell had been delving into the first-aid box, his personal survival kit, and lamenting the fact that he hadn't been able to launch the rubber raft in which was stored several days' food rations, water and most important, a thermal-foil survival blanket. He looked up and his gaze encompassed them all. "You should've emptied your bladders before it got dark and the storm got worse."

"Now you remind us," Rebecca said with unalloyed sarcasm.

"Common sense should've—"

"Well I don't have any common sense!" she cried. "Who would in a situation like this?"

"Cripes. You don't have to have another tantrum."

Rebecca expended great effort to withhold a reply.

"I really have to go," warned Molly.

Parnell dragged himself to his feet, stooping to keep from thrusting through the roof. He ducked his head out the opening. Wind-driven snow stung his face. Visibility was about five yards. He expelled a dour sigh. "All right, bundle up. It's best if we all go at the same time."

Rebecca was momentarily flustered. "We'll need some privacy."

Parnell shook his head. "Damn it, this ain't the Waldorf. Follow me and stay close. I know people who got lost in snow storms and froze to death ten feet from their own front door." He didn't actually, but he'd read about them. He didn't believe in lying unless the lie benefitted all concerned. Or saved his own neck. In this instance he figured both eventualities were covered.

"I take back every nice thing I said about you," Rebecca said as she leaned into the wind.

"I never pay any attention to female chatter anyhow." Parnell was stung. In swimming the lake he'd been gallant, selfless. And almost froze his pecker off.

It just went to prove what he knew all along. Women were inconsiderate, insincere and rude.

Rebecca fell in line last. It was a most unpleasant experience. The boys had an easier go of it than she and Molly did. They, at least could lean into the shelter of a tree. The design of the female body precluded that. But because of the dark and the thickness of the forest, she did manage a modicum of privacy. It was too cold to dawdle.

It seemed they had no more gotten settled around the fire again when the storm rose in pitch. The trees surrounding the shelter blunted the wind, but still it whistled a steady discordant note, and above their heads the flimsy limbs creaked.

"Tomorrow I'll fix up a latrine of some sort," Parnell mumbled.

"Thank you," Rebecca replied stiffly, averting her gaze. The snow and forest had not hidden her as much as she had thought! To keep him from dwelling on it she asked, "Can we sleep without our shoes, you think?" She was concerned about Molly. The corrective shoes the child had to wear were heavy. Taking them off was always a relief.

"I wouldn't recommend it." Who knew what would happen during the night, Parnell thought. The shelter might fall apart, or catch fire. In a race for safety, shoes would be left behind. He wouldn't want to put odds on their survival if they had to go barefoot.

Rebecca searched through Molly's tote for the Lubriderm lotion then pulled Molly into her lap and began unlacing the unwieldy shoes. "A few minutes won't hurt. I'll massage your feet."

"Scrappy! I forgot Scrappy!" Yancy yelped. He scrambled over several pairs of legs and past Rebecca. Parnell caught him as he tried to lurch through the opening. He counted heads.

"We're all here."

"Not Scrappy," wailed Yancy. "I tied him to a bush while I was—"

Parnell was nonplussed. "Who the hell is Scrappy?" He looked at Rebecca. "Don't tell me, you smuggled a damned dog or something aboard."

"Scrappy is—"

"He's gonna freeze!" the child cried hysterically.

"I told you about Scrappy," Jonesy reminded.

"I'll go get him," Santee volunteered.

"Stay put!" bawled Parnell. "Just calm down. I'll get him." His eyes rested on Rebecca. "What am I looking for?"

She took a deep breath. "A horse."

Parnell was certain he wasn't hearing right. "A who?"

"A horse."

Jonesy leaned over and whispered in Parnell's ear. Rebecca watched the pilot. He seemed to sag. His face took on the look of a starving man invited to dine on boiled sheep's eyes. His gaze shifted from the panic-stricken Yancy to lock on her. Silently she implored him to accept the idea if not the fact of Scrappy.

"You see why I don't like women and kids?" he groused convincingly. But in a far corner of his mind was the vague remembrance of his own youth and the friendly cowboy warrior he'd often conjured up as a playmate. Though he'd sure as hell never told anybody about him! The little leg he grasped in his hand was thin as a stick. The youngster's eyes were rounded like a soulful puppy's, tears wet on long lashes. The expression on Rebecca's face was no less appealing. Shoot!

He crawled out the opening, stomped around the shelter once and reemerged. Agitated, his face flushed and feeling utterly the fool, he passed imaginary reins to Yancy.

"Here!" he choked. "In the future...in the future, act more responsible." Sensing everyone's undivided attention, he said, "Hell!"

"Thank you," Rebecca told him, deciding it was just possible to like the man—though she knew there was a degree of rationalization in her thinking.

"Don't thank me! I don't like doing things to get thanked for."

"Yes, Captain," she answered, lamblike.

He gave her a dirty look, then settled himself on his side, and began rooting through the kit once again.

Rebecca watched him for a few seconds. No man that she knew would have indulged a six-year-old and gone out in the midst of a snowstorm to pretend to find an imaginary creature. She decided there was a kindness in him that was not readily apparent. True, he was bossy, he could turn the air blue with pungent language and he found fault with all that she said or did, but if one weighed all that against his actual deeds, he presented an entirely different picture. For all his bluff and bluster he was simply a macho romantic, she reflected, and scared to death he'd be found out.

"What are you smiling at?" Parnell snapped.

Rebecca jerked. "Who, me? Was I smiling?"

"Yes, at me," he accused, all male suspicion.

"An oversight on my part. It won't happen again."

"You looked happy." He didn't want to let it go. He thought she was laughing at him.

"I'm not happy. I'm miserable." She tried to fit her features into an acceptable image of wretchedness, keeping her eyes downcast lest the pilot read the truth in them. For a moment she was tempted to tell him she had his number. That she saw right through his facade. Better not, she thought. He might fall apart.

FINALLY, ROLLED UP in their coats and huddling together for warmth, the children slept. Totes were used as pillows while extra clothing was used to soften the knobby brush bedding. Nearer the fire Rebecca sat Indian-fashion upon her own coat.

The shelter smelled of wood smoke. Under other circumstances, she thought, it would've been pleasant with the wood crackling and the coals glowing red.

The pilot was still awake, his eyes narrowed to slits. Rebecca sensed his gaze upon her. She suddenly felt that awkwardness of being in a small elevator and unable to evade scrutiny by the only other occupant. Which made her wonder what she looked like.

The empty juice cartons were lined in foil. She tore open two, filled them with a handful of snow and put them near the fire. When the snow had melted she used her scarf to dip into the lukewarm water to wash her face and hands. Her hair was a mass of tangles. She brushed it. There was something so normal, so everyday in the act that Rebecca lost herself in the pleasure of it.

From across the fire pit Parnell watched her with a set, tense expression on his face. The flames cast patterns of golden flecks in her eyes so that he could not tell exactly their color. After several brush strokes, her lids fluttered and her long crisp lashes closed, leaving him guessing still about their color.

Each time she raised and lowered her arm one voluptuous breast rose and fell with it. He could tell she was voluptuous because she had buttoned her sweater and the outline was there for any but a blind man to see. The way she sat, the lift and fall of her arm hinted at a languid sensuality that burned just beneath her surface. A weak man would challenge that sensuality, Parnell thought. But not him. He was strong. Then he discovered he was holding his breath; his heart was jumping against his ribs like a caged animal. Cripes! She was getting to him. Before he could force himself to look away her eyes opened and she looked directly at him. She lifted her chin and held his gaze for just long enough and then turned her head unhurriedly to set aside the brush. Before he could decide whether her look was invitation or disdain, she spoke.

"You don't have anything for a pillow. Want to use this?" She passed him a folded garment out of her suitcase.

He debated acceptance. If he refused, no telling what she'd think. First rule in war games was never let the enemy know he had gained an advantage. "Thanks," he muttered and jammed it under his head. Immediately her scent filled his nostrils. Body musk and something flowery, lilac maybe. He hadn't smelled a woman's scent since he couldn't remember when. It conjured up all sorts of erotic images in his mind's eye.

"Good night," Rebecca called softly from the nest she'd created for herself next to Molly.

"Same to you," Parnell replied tersely, promising himself that the next time she began preening for his benefit, he'd ignore her entirely. His rear ached. He welcomed the pain. It kept him distracted from the woman smell lodged beneath his head.

THE SOUND, thick and gravelly, came coiling into her sleep. It continued for some time before Rebecca paid any attention to it and realized that it was a voice, and that she had slept through a night she had expected to be sleepless. Then she also became aware of the stab of cold and the buzz of numbness in her body. For an instant she felt the weight of a huge stillness. The wind had stopped.

The gravelly noise started again. She opened her eyes in the shadowed dimness.

The children lay body to body, not stirring, but snuffling softly so that she knew each was alive. The noise was coming from Parnell. He was on his feet, but bent over. The smoldering coals gave off little light. She had to raise her head to get a better view of him. His pants were down about his knees, and he was plucking at his underwear. All the while issuing low guttural moans.

"What's the matter with you?" she whispered.

Parnell jerked, straightened. His head hit the lodgepole. "Oh, damn! Ouch. Cripes. Mind your own business."

Rebecca sat up. "Why are your pants down? Were you doing something vulgar?"

"That was nasty and uncalled for." He stopped struggling with his pants, dropped down, rolled on his belly and pulled his coat over his head. The noises low in his throat began again, but were muffled somewhat by the coat. Rebecca crawled around to his side. She lifted a corner of the coat.

"I didn't mean to accuse you of anything. Why are you making those terrible sounds?"

"Leave me alone."

"Are you hurting?"

"I'm fine," came in a strangely anguished tone.

"Are you coming down with the flu? Is it your fanny? Let me have a look."

"Hey!" But Rebecca had already lifted his coat. The lighting was too shadowy for her to see much. She put her hand on him and trailed it cautiously over his backside. At her touch she felt his muscles contract, which in turn caused a gruff moan to escape his lips.

"Your underwear got stiff and stuck to you."

"Tell me something I don't know."

"Will you stop being a smart ass? Suppose this becomes infected and you die of blood poisoning?"

"Right now, dying looks good."

"Oh, hush and let me think."

Her hand was under his sweater, resting on the small of his back. It was cool on his skin. He could pick out its shape. Despite the pain radiating out below it, he felt an involuntary tingle of rising pleasure and anticipation.

"I'll heat some water like I did earlier," Rebecca decided. "Then pour it on warm and peel your underwear back. At least far enough that I can—"

"No." There was no doubt in Parnell's mind of the sense of what she was proposing, but he just couldn't see himself lying there, allowing her to administer to him. When he'd been unconscious, he hadn't had a choice. But now . . . If she was a nurse, it'd be different.

"Now, see here . . ." Rebecca projected the tone she used with the children when they were being stubborn.

"I don't want you fiddling with me," Parnell said.

His words sank in and registered. After a moment Rebecca trilled, "Fiddling with you? Fiddling with you . . . as in 'fooling around'?"

"It's been known to happen."

Rebecca leaned back and rested her derriere on her heels. "You're undoubtedly the most arrogant, the most vile, the most unhinged man I have ever met. I wouldn't be interested in you if you were shaved and dressed in a tuxedo!"

Parnell tried to discern her features, but her back was to the fire and he couldn't. She sounded serious enough. There was some comfort and safety in that. "You might change your mind," he suggested, probing the depth of her sincerity. A man had to be on guard against the fickle way a woman's mind worked, or else find himself committed to a life of misery without even opening his mouth!

Rebecca was dumbfounded. The man was so dense he couldn't even be insulted. "I don't even want to be friends with you. All I want is for you to get us back to Boise. Then I hope I never see you again in my life!"

"Oh, well, that's all right then." Satisfied, he laid his head back down on the makeshift pillow. The smell of it haunted him but he was certain of his resistance now. "There's some salve in the first-aid kit. And, be careful."

Rebecca built up the fire, repeatedly filling the juice packs with snow. The first that was melted, she and Parnell drank. The thermos had not been among the things he had retrieved and she mourned its loss. It still had several cups of coffee in it.

Bit by bit she dampened the longjohns and separated the fabric from his flayed skin, rolling it down inch by inch. Parnell put a twig in his mouth to bite down on against the pain. He kept biting it in two and finally just gave over to issuing small gasps.

Rebecca's fury at him stayed with her until his buttocks were revealed. They were so flayed, so raw that unbidden compassion rose of its own accord. "This will probably sting," she said quietly, her hands poised to lather him with the ointment.

"I can handle it."

"Here goes," Rebecca said and began to massage it in.

"Cripes!" Parnell yelped. Her hands were small, yet strong at kneading his flesh and there was that lingering womanly musk smell in his nose. After a minute he began to groan softly.

There was something in the sound of his "oohs" and "aaahs" that made Rebecca stop. She looked at his face. His eyes were closed. His full lips had lost their tenseness. The salve was a topical anesthetic laced with an antibiotic. It was supposed to relieve his pain, but still...the look on his face gave her pause. Testing him, she spread another layer of the salve, softly stroking his lower back and buttocks. "Does that feel better?" she cooed with artificial sweetness.

"Wonderful," he breathed, mesmerized by the first thrilling shock of stimulation.

"I'll just bet it does! You pervert."

Parnell's eyes flew open. He looked at her guiltily. "It was the pain going away. I swear!"

"Men! You're all alike. I dare you to turn over and pull your pants up in front of me."

Parnell cursed his body and stalled for time. "You have a dirty mind."

"I recognize arousal when I see it!"

"Is there anything for breakfast?"

Rebecca spun around. All five of the children were sitting up, eyes round. Her face flamed.

Parnell used the distraction to yank his underwear and pants up.

The survival kit held hard bars of bittersweet chocolate. He rubbed his hands with snow then broke the chocolate apart. "We'll wash these down with hot water," he said.

"I wish we had scrambled eggs and big thick sausages," said Jonesy.

"Shut up," said Santee. "That's the worst thing you can do when you're hungry. Anyhow, wishing ain't never got us anything, has it?"

"Stop being so cynical," Rebecca told him. The bit of chocolate melted on her tongue. It was old, terrible tasting. But as she washed it down she felt energy renewed. She straightened her legs and arched in a slow catlike stretch to release the stiffness in her body. Parnell's eyes swiveled toward her. Her gaze struck his, her brain named the expression he wore as a cow-eyed leer. She held her head at a haughty angle which emphasized the strong independent line of mouth and jaw.

"Wipe that idea right out of your mind," she said, voice clipped and dry as dust. But a small voice at the back of her mind was reminding her of how his hardmuscled back had felt beneath her fingers, how the fright within her had been comforted by the intimate, physical contact.

Parnell looked hastily away. To his dismay, the image of her stayed with him. He muttered something indecipherable, shrugged into his jacket and lunged out of the shelter into the grainy silver light of predawn.

"Are we gonna be rescued today?" asked Yancy.

"I hope so," Rebecca replied fervently. "Oh, I hope so."

"A smart person could make out fine in these woods," said Santee. "There're wild animals to trap and skin and eat. Probably fish in the lake . . ."

Rebecca started to remind him that they weren't on a scouting trip, but changed her mind. If his ideas occupied him and the other children, that was all to the good.

"I guess I'd better figure the place out," said Nicholas. "I was too tired last night." He engaged Santee in his clock routine to define the outline of his temporary home from where he sat.

Parnell appeared in the shelter. "Everybody out," he ordered, stooping to bank the fire. "It's stopped snowing. We can stamp out an SOS down by the lake." He reached for the survival kit and withdrew the spray can of orange fluorescent paint. Fluorescent had been Uncle Henry's idea. "Better than dye," he'd once said. He'd thought if ever needed, it'd at least carry some shine beyond dusk and be visible from the sky. Parnell hoped the man was right.

"You think somebody's out looking for us now?" Rebecca asked hopefully.

"I know they're looking. Let's just hope they look our way."

"Which is?"

"I'll figure that out later."

Mittens and caps had been left behind in the urgent exit of the plane or lost in the rush. Now the morning air chilled their ears and scalps, chapped their hands and made their lungs ache. The snow was deep, piled in drifts, knee-high on Rebecca, but almost waist-high on the younger children. Already Rebecca was anticipating having to dry them out, warm them. As if to enhance her dread Molly gave forth a phlegmy cough.

When they came out of the trees atop the incline that led down to the lake, Rebecca gasped. "Where's the plane?" Somehow it was a link to rescue, to her past, to the future. She couldn't bear its loss.

"Snow's covered it," Parnell told her, pointing.

Rebecca followed the direction of his arm. She saw it then, the ungainly shape. The nose looked only like a giant snow-covered rock, the wings barely discernible. "Will anyone be able to tell what it is from the air?"

The dawn light cast pearly highlights on her skin and shaded the hollows of her face. Her hair was loose, falling about her shoulders. There was a look on her face of unadorned vulnerability. It was something new for Parnell to think a woman vulnerable. He knew it was a vital ingredient in men, albeit a thing to be hidden at all cost. A too-vulnerable man in the clutches of the wrong woman was a goner. Yet, recognizing the unguarded emotion in Rebecca made him shiver. She was very pale, scared. Whether she wanted it or not, he decided, she needed his protection, from the elements, from fear.

"From the air, it'll look like just what it is," he lied. "Any pilot worth his salt will be able to pick out that nose cone from five thousand feet. Don't worry."

There was an element she had not heretofore heard in his voice. Rebecca glanced at him quickly, but he'd already turned away and was directing the children. "The incline works to our advantage," he was saying. "The SOS will stand out like a sign on a barn."

Nicholas kept marching out on the curves. "Damn it!" Parnell yelled, looking behind himself to view their progress. "Stay inside the line."

"Well, I can't see, you know," Nicholas yelled back. "Get onto Molly, it's her coattail I'm hanging on to."

"You better not fuss at me. I'm the littlest. And anyhow, I'll cry." Then she sat down in the trampled snow and did just that.

"Oh hell!" He signaled to Rebecca. "Do something."

"Well, we're all freezing. Can't we have a fire down here?" Her feet were so cold she couldn't keep her mind on anything else.

Parnell glanced at the early-morning sky. It was a sullen gray. Somewhere to the south or east of them air-rescue teams were reviewing the weather window, charting search grids. The smoke from a small fire would dissipate, be invisible. Once the air grid was flown it might be days before the grid was checked again, if ever. The bright orange SOS might be their only chance.

"After the signal is laid out, I'll build a fire, not before." He stomped his way back to where Molly sat.

"Stop sniveling and get back in line." He searched for something to threaten her with. "If you don't, you're going to turn into a wart."

The other kids giggled. Molly began to wail in earnest.

Rebecca rained verbal abuse on Parnell for raining verbal abuse on Molly. Santee crabbed back to the girl and talked to her quietly. Molly's eyes got huge, her tears stopped. She got to her feet.

When the four-foot-high, two-foot-deep SOS was finally completed, Parnell insisted the sides be pounded into a hard icy surface. In the event it snowed again, he believed he'd be able to shovel out the new snow, preserving the signal.

"You did good," he told them all when they were warming their hands at the fire he'd promised to build.

Rebecca surged with hope. The bright orange letters looked so reassuring she silently forgave Parnell the roughshod way he'd hounded her and the children. She moved to his side and touched him on his arm. "What now?" she asked.

The weight of her hand was featherlight. Parnell felt a sudden warmth that she'd touched it. As casually as he could manage, as if it were the most natural thing in the world, he placed his own hand over hers while he searched the leaden sky. It was empty of bird, fly or plane.

"We wait," he said.

6

"YOU KNOW WHAT I wish I had," Jonesy said with a sigh. "A foot-long hot dog. Fried crisp and dipped in mustard and covered with so much chili it dripped out both ends."

"My mouth's watering for cinnamon toast," said Yancy.

"Double-stuffed Oreos!" piped Molly.

"I'm so hungry I'd even eat oatmeal," said Nicholas. "And, I hate the stuff!"

Rebecca visualized the food. Her throat convulsed in a spasmodic swallowing reflex. Hunger was quickly becoming a relentless enemy. Lunch had consisted of a tiny bit of hard chocolate. And they'd sucked the last of it for supper. To fortify themselves against the lingering sense of emptiness, the children had drunk so much warm water their stomaches bulged. Afterward Molly had complained. Rebecca suspected colic. Yet the warmed water in her own stomach seemed to drug her.

"If there's fishing line in your rucksack," Santee said to Parnell, "I could set rabbit snares tomorrow."

"There's some in the plane. Maybe we'll be able to get it in the morning."

Rebecca didn't like the implication of their conversation. "Surely we'll be found tomorrow."

"Weather permitting and depending on how they've set up search grids," Parnell replied. He'd studied his charts. He had the terrible suspicion that the storm had pushed them much father south and east than he'd first thought. He knew the air rescue teams would chart search grids working from his filed flight plan. But the skies had remained empty all day. The logical conclusion was that he had landed entirely outside the far reaches of any supposed coordinates.

He suspected the frozen lake was little more than a shallow sink; dry some years, wet others, for there was no creek or river feeding into it. Nor could he locate the lake on the charts.

He caught Rebecca staring intently at him. She'd have to be told the situation sooner or later. He decided on later, warned off by the emotional intensity of her expression. He gave her his most winning grin.

"Get some rest," he suggested.

His attempt at a lopsided smile startled Rebecca. It changed his whole face, taking the menace out of it and somehow making the formidable features in his bearded, craggy face appear aristocratic and sensitive. Had the man been clean shaven, she might even find him attractive. Now that was a stupid irrelevant thought, she chastised herself. It was only that hunger was so unspeakable. It was making her imagination soar.

"Santa Claus will find us for sure," said Molly. "Santee said he'd see our SOS and bring our presents here."

"Santa Claus!" Rebecca put her arm around the child. "Christmas is two weeks away yet. We'll be home long before Santa arrives."

"But if we're not," the child insisted.

"We will be," Rebecca said tersely, and looked to the pilot to back her up. But his face was hidden in the shadows and he said nothing. To keep her uncertainty at bay, she kept busy; she added wood to the fire, massaged Molly's feet, invented a word game to occupy the youngsters for an hour. They became drowsy and slept. Rebecca tucked her own coat around Molly. The child's cough had worsened in the afternoon. She didn't want her chilled during the night when the fire burned low.

But Rebecca couldn't sleep. She felt the need of assurance, had an urge to talk. She moved to sit nearer the fire next to Parnell.

"Back at the orphanage," she said conversationally, "if I'd ordered them to bed this early, I'd've had to field twenty different excuses."

"They're tired."

"And you?" she questioned. All through the long gray day, the pilot and Santee had kept a vigil near the SOS. She and the others had been driven back to the shelter in the early afternoon by the sudden drop in temperature. As if nature meant to remind her of the cold, she felt a sudden draft on her cheek.

"I'm used to long hours," Parnell answered.

He was melting snow in the foil boxes and leaned forward to turn them. The foil was wearing out, Rebecca noticed. Managing the most mundane ablutions took extraordinary measures. She had tried to brush her teeth with snow and toothpaste, and found it too painful. A flimsy three-sided lean-to had been slapped together to serve as a bathroom, tissue from her cosmetic case used sparingly. Still, they had very little of anything to go on with. And no food at all now.

"What're we going to do?" she whispered. She knew her voice quavered, knew it revealed her fears. She couldn't help it.

Parnell reached behind him and tugged his kit forward. "I was saving this, but I think you need a nip." He dug around inside and brought out a pint of whiskey. "Not the best," he said of the Jim Beam, "but it'll help you sleep."

Whiskey! The sight of it brought back old memories, reminders of bitter disappointments. Her father's indulgence had been the bane of her childhood. He'd been a charming drunk, but a drunk nevertheless and not dependable. It frightened Rebecca to think that the pilot had that same flaw. In their circumstances a mind dulled by liquor would be disastrous.

"If you'd had food in that kit," she said pointedly, "if you'd been more responsible... You should've had—"

A strange gleam of belligerence began spreading in Parnell's eyes. He held up a protesting hand, "Spare me the lecture. There're some sea rations in the plane. I couldn't get to them. This is my private survival kit so to speak." He tore the seal on the bottle and took a long swig. Rebecca heard him swallow. Ten seconds ticked by in utter silence before Parnell said, "If it's food you want, then food you'll have. I'll go after it in the morning."

The rush of anger died in Rebecca. "You think the lake will be frozen over enough to hold you?"

"Hope so."

"Wait a minute," she said, clarity dawning. "You can't be thinking about swimming again. It's colder now than when we... Suppose... You can't. No! I won't let you."

Warmed by the whiskey, he mocked softly. "There're some things you might stop me from doing, but that's not one of them." His eyes changed to shrewd reflection as he held out the bottle toward her. "Have a sociable drink."

"No thank you," she said stiffly.

"Suit yourself." He put the whiskey away.

"What else is in that kit?"

"A blister pack of painkillers." He paused. "A gun."

Rebecca sucked in her breath. "With bullets?"

"Wouldn't do me any good without them."

"But, why?"

"Fear of fire, I guess."

"You're not making any sense. You're already drunk." She remembered he hadn't shared in the last bit of chocolate. "You shouldn't drink on an empty stomach."

"Rebecca," he said softly, using her name for the first time and liking the shape of it on his lips, "if you have a problem with liquor, don't lay it on me."

She stiffened and paled. "I don't have a problem, but swilling whiskey never solves anything."

"You have a husband who gets drunk and beats you?"

"No. I had a father who was drunk the first twelve years of my life."

"And then?"

"And then my brother was born."

"I guess I'm dense, but I don't see the connection."

"My father stopped drinking because he had a son to raise."

She had never resented her brother, but he had grown up in a charmed environment, exactly the opposite of her own youth. The sad thing was that whatever he asked for, he got. Now at twenty, he had the idea the world owed him. It wasn't until she began to work with the orphans that she'd realized how spoiled he'd become.

"Ah. Your father didn't appreciate you. He hurt your feelings and you blame it on the liquor. Women think crazy. I've known that for a month of Sundays." His expression changed, as if he'd had a sudden anxious thought. "You got anybody back in Boise who'd be raising heck with the authorities to get on with the search?"

"Just Abigail."

"No husband?" He paced his tone with a feigned hopefulness.

Rebecca took the bait. "No. I had a husband. But he was selfish. He found me boring. Anyway, he's married again. He couldn't care less. He'd probably be thrilled with the prospect of my...disappearance. I was his biggest mistake. He doesn't like being reminded."

There was a cunning satisfaction in Parnell's expression, as if he'd known all along which layers to peel back to reveal an inner core. "I don't think you're boring. Quarrelsome, maybe."

She'd said too much, Rebecca realized, and on all the wrong topics. What her life had been was none of his business. "We were talking about your gun."

He shrugged out of his jacket, stretched languidly to take his weight on his hip, wincing as he crossed his legs. "One thing a pilot doesn't like to worry about is being trapped in a cockpit fire. Fire's a terrible thing—not exactly quick, if you know what I mean. That's the reason for the gun." He checked the foil boxes, sipped from them. Held the last one out to Rebecca.

Rebecca scrutinized Parnell, but saw nothing behind the veil of his dark eyes. "You mean it's to kill yourself?"

"To end a horrible misery should the occasion arise."

Rebecca glanced down at the length of him. She didn't know if what he proposed was a strength or a weakness. She drank the water, gathered up the boxes and cached them. "Suppose the plane had caught fire when we crashed?"

"It didn't."

"But if it had?"

"It didn't. And anyway, we didn't crash in the literal sense of the word." With the hope that she'd recognize the skill it had taken, he added, "It was a textbook gears-up landing."

"But then the plane sank."

Effort wasted, Parnell decided, disconsolate. He wadded up the flannel gown of hers that was serving him as pillow. "In case you're still worried, I never drink to excess."

Rebecca averted her face. "I guess I was out of line."

"You're different, I'll hand you that."

The comment begged her curiosity. "What do you mean?"

"You're the first woman I've ever met who almost apologized for being wrong."

"You're the first man I've ever met who looks like a derelict, but isn't—almost."

Parnell grinned. "Comments like that might drive me to shave."

"Why don't you?"

"Couldn't bear up under the adoration."

"You're sick," she said, her tone as chilly as the fingers of cold creeping into the shelter. "All you are is another arrogant male, full of himself. You need a lesson in humility."

"I suppose you're just the person to give me the lesson."

"Not me, I couldn't care less."

"You're breaking my heart." He yawned a long comfortable yawn.

"As if you had one."

"Now that hurts. You don't hear me saying I couldn't care less, do you?" He reached up and put his hand on her shoulder. She tensed, but did not pull away.

"Lie back," he coaxed, arranging the brush and bracken to accommodate her. "You're getting cold. I can see you shivering."

"I'm all right." He was just feigning compassion, she thought.

"You look a bit unstrung to me." Then, softly, as if it were an afterthought he said, "You did pretty well handling things today."

His praise was so welcome that she did not resist when he tugged her down and covered her with his jacket.

Parnell wondered at the gentle streak that had surfaced in himself. He'd never known he possessed it. On the other hand, there'd never been anyone in his life to encourage it or draw it out. "How's your elbow?"

"My what? Oh. Oh, it's fine. How about your— you?"

"Better, much better."

When he thought she was soundly asleep he cautiously slipped beneath his coat next to her. She didn't move; he felt absurdly pleased with himself. After ten minutes he inched his arm across her abdomen. Her head was just beneath his chin, and even with the thickness of clothing her slender body seemed to fit exactly right with his own. But hell, he thought, that didn't mean anything. Except maybe that the whiskey had gone to his head.

He felt a stirring of life in his groin. Cripes! That was twice in twelve hours she'd caused his libido to act up. For a while he basked in the sensation. When it got too much for him to endure he spent a woesome twenty minutes overruling it.

IT TOOK ALL HER SELF-CONTROL for Rebecca to pretend sleep. She didn't dare move, yet her senses were uncommonly alert. The fire crackled as the wood turned to ash, she picked out the soft uneven snores of the children, and in the greater silence beyond the shelter, she could hear snow-laden limbs creaking beneath the weight.

She breathed in the oil and soap and sweat scent of Parnell. When she'd had her fill, she eased her throat and let her breath out slowly. A glorious glow suffused her tired body and lightning quivers ran to the tips of her toes, her fingers, and she thought, I can't let this go on. But it did, and she liked it.

On the face of it she couldn't understand how she'd let the pilot maneuver her into lying beside him. The universal need for companionship in a crisis, she supposed.

No, that was a lie. The touch of another human being, the fact that he wanted to touch her was exhilarating.

Oh, she thought, unreasonably near tears, she'd had such a small, dull life. Thirty-two years of it. She ached for affection. She always had. It was her Achilles heel.

Since her divorce she hadn't looked at or encouraged any man's attention. She missed the sense of belonging, missed having someone to love, someone to fuss over. To fuss at. If a woman had a natural inclination to nag, and Rebecca was sure she did, the pilot was a wonderful target. He had so many flaws, you could pick a different one for each day of the week and not run out for months.

And, he'd never change his ways, he was too lackadaisical. She was as certain of that as she was of her propensity for scolding.

In spite of the wretchedness of the situation, perhaps even on account of it, maybe Destiny was playing her a fair hand for a change.

Listen to yourself, you idiot! she mused. What happened to a brain when the body was starving? Did an empty stomach make for crazy ideas?

She felt the sudden swell of Parnell against her hip and bit back the gasp that rose in her throat. There was that to consider, too. As if they didn't have enough problems!

Crazy or not, it was nice to know she could stir a man to passion. Oh! It was lovely to cuddle, be comforted and feel protected. There was a humming in her breasts, a heat in her thighs. Dear God, she thought prayerfully, how she needed someone who needed her.

Ingenuously, as though shifting in her sleep, she fitted herself more snugly into the curve of his body. She felt the whole of him go rigid, sensed he was holding his breath.

First thing in the morning, she decided, she'd insist upon checking his injuries. It was the least she could do.

"NO THANKS, I'm fine," Parnell said, refusing to look at her. "How about letting me borrow that toothpaste. My mouth tastes like a stable."

She squeezed the paste onto his finger. "You don't have to act shy, not now."

He shot her a glare of high suspicion. Rebecca countered it. "Look, the sun is shining. I'll send the kids outside. It won't take a minute. Supposing you get an infection?"

Oh, yeah, he thought, but supposing he got something else? Like a pecker that stood up and waved like a flagpole. He couldn't take the chance. She was already bringing something out of him. Something he'd never felt before. A tug in his gut. In the light of day, he remembered he didn't like women. And why. Anyway, she'd made him miserable all night what with her hair tickling his nose, and smelling like shampoo and wood smoke. Not to mention curling up against him like she had. "My drawers go up and down like a snap," he said. "I don't need doctoring."

"Hey, Rebecca! Look at this," Jonesy said wonderingly. "I had to tighten my belt a notch. I'm shrinking."

"Yeah, well," Parnell shot at the overweight youngster, "you can afford it." He glanced outside. The sun was casting golden fingers on the snow, chasing the shadows back.

"I found some rabbit tracks out by the lean-to," Santee said as he emerged into the shelter leading Nicholas. "If we get that fishing line, I can set a snare. Roasted rabbit sounds good, don't it?"

"Roasted anything sounds good to me," said Jonesy. "My stomach's growling so much I could eat a horse."

Yancy screamed. "No!"

"Geez, I didn't mean Scrappy," Jonesy said.

"You're not supposed to eat horses," wailed Yancy.

"Hey anybody, my zipper's stuck, my fingers're too cold to get it uncaught," said Nicholas.

"My throat hurts," whined Molly.

"Let me outta here," said Parnell, exiting so fast he knocked over two of the foil boxes.

"Look what you just did, you clumsy ox!" Rebecca hollered after him.

Parnell bent down and talked through the opening. "We're going to be found today. We have to be. Another twelve hours of this and I'm going to be a basket case. Quiet down those kids before you let them come anywhere near me."

Rebecca crawled through the opening and stood to face him. Her breath misted the air. "There're just being kids. Good ones, I might add. They've hardly complained. Whose fault is it that we're cooped up here anyway?"

"Your own. I told you, you're bad luck."

"I don't know how I could have possibly thought you're anything other than what you look like: an unkempt Neanderthal with an underdeveloped brain."

"Oh, we're into name-calling again. Well, lady, have I got a name for you. Tease! Cuddling up to me last night. I know what you're after."

Rebecca's eyes went stony. "You don't have anything I want. I've seen you, remember? Besides, you insisted I lie down beside you."

"I had a weak moment. I felt sorry for you."

"Just go on down to the lake and drown yourself. See if I miss you."

"Stick it in your ear," he said, and stalked off.

In various states of undress the children had lined up outside the shelter to listen. Their expressions were wary. Facing them, Rebecca felt a stab of guilt. They were all from broken homes, abandoned by family or circumstances. She was supposed to be doing better by them than what they'd come from. "I'm sorry," she said. "The captain is just a bit upset. Inside, all of you. Let's get cleaned up and bundled up. I'm sure we'll be rescued today. We'll want to look neat."

She made everybody brush their teeth and hair, switch socks from one foot to another, put on a clean shirt. She fed them warm water and made Molly take a pill out of Parnell's kit. The gun was gone. At least he wasn't stupid enough to leave it lying about, she thought. But he was stupid in every other way. He thought her a tease. Well, he was right. But he'd started it.

"If we weren't already lost," said Yancy forlornly, "me and Scrappy would run away."

"I wish my mommy was here," said Molly.

Rebecca kneeled down by the girl. "She's in heaven, sweetheart. You know that."

"I know God took her. But he can get his own mommy. I want mine back."

Santee hefted the hatchet. "Me and Jonesy can chop wood, Rebecca. Okay?"

"Don't go far, I don't want you two lost."

"We already are that."

"No. The searchers know we're out here."

"Not for sure they don't. They probably think we're dead." He sounded as if being lost forever suited him just fine.

"Well, we aren't and we're not going to be. Stop talking like that. You want to chop wood, go do it. But Santee, be careful!"

"That toothpaste tasted pretty good," said Nicholas.

Rebecca closed her eyes. Please let us be found today, she prayed. Please.

She kept the younger children with her as long as she could. But the glistening light of the weak sun drew them outside. And once outside, they wanted to play; make snowballs and snowmen. Yancy hit upon using the mail cart lid for a sled. They yelled and squealed up and down the incline, too often getting perilously close to destroying the SOS. They left their shirts and sweaters buttoned up to the top to ward off the cold, but left jackets open for better movement. They were far more durable than she, Rebecca mused and gave up trying to keep them bundled.

Parnell had built a small fire down close to the lake edge by a jumble of bulky rocks that had many ages ago tumbled down from a higher point on the mountain. His company she didn't want, Rebecca told herself, but the fire beckoned and she walked toward it. Studiously ignoring Parnell, she warmed her hands.

It seemed to her they were on the floor of the world, the curve of the land was upward, upward, upward. No birds flew, deer had moved to lower slopes, bears hibernated. Lucky bears, Rebecca thought, sleeping through winter on full stomachs in some warm cozy den. She listened for the sound of the hatchet. It came faintly, muted by the forest and the snow.

Parnell was backed up to the fire, his hands clasped behind him, his head tilted skyward.

He was very much aware of Rebecca's nearness, but he was determined that she, not he, would break the silence.

Rebecca's eyes kept straying to Parnell's wide back. It occurred to her that she wasn't as fearful as she might have been had she been in the wilds with a lesser man. In spite of their differences she was beginning to trust the pilot. Actually, trust!

Perhaps she was even falling for him. What a stupid idea! Just look at him. His beard stubble had grown thicker, his hair was in wild disarray and he still slouched inside his clothes as if they were old friends fallen on hard times. She had to keep reminding herself that they were thrown so intimately together by an unforeseeable event; that the sensation of wanting to cling to him was only natural. Fear was as much her constant companion as the bitter cold.

And the fluttering in the pit of your stomach? a small voice asked. Hunger, Rebecca answered. Still, she couldn't bear his silence another moment.

"Do you think they'll come today? The rescue planes?" she asked.

Parnell turned and gazed at her. He felt his resolution sway slightly. Her eyes were huge in her face. Gray. He wouldn't forget. The cold put color in her cheeks, highlighting the fine structure of cheekbone and brow. He felt again the strange tugging in his gut that had nothing to do with lack of food. If the feeling crept any lower he was going to be in big trouble. Cripes! He was turning into a mewling seventeen-year-old.

Rebecca misread the signals he was sending. "You think we're going to die here, don't you?"

"No, I don't think that at all. There may be no planes though. Sometimes everything is done by computer."

"What?"

"If the ELT is working they'll take a fix, estimating latitude and longitude, then send in a ground crew."

"A ground crew? From where? How long would that take? Parnell, we're hungry."

He didn't miss the use of his name. He liked hearing it. To hide his pleasure, he glanced at the sky. The sun would be at its zenith in a few hours. "It could take a few days, but it's a sure thing." He hoped.

"What about the rations on the plane? The ice? Have you checked it? Will it hold you?"

"Not yet. By midnight maybe." He watched her face crumble. She looked so small and defenseless standing in snow up to her knees, the mountain at her back dwarfing her. He couldn't help himself. He went to her and folded his arms around her.

She let her weight sink against him; felt the warmth of his embrace and buried her face in the shoulder of his jacket.

"I suppose you're just feeling sorry for me again," she said.

Parnell cleared his throat. "Well—no. Not exactly." He noted she fit in his arms standing up as well as she had lying down. Was that an omen?

She moved her head; he could feel her breath on his neck. "What then—exactly?" she said.

"Hell, I don't know." He didn't have any words for it. She was happening to him. He didn't have any explanation for it. But she was looking up at him. He had to say something. That was the way it was with a woman. You had to give her reasons, logic. A reason came to him. "I think it's sex."

She jerked away.

"You asked! I told you. What was I supposed to say?"

"Nothing. Just nothing."

"Damn it! You get stiff-necked over every little thing. If I was married to you, which I'm not, but if I was, I'd quit you, too. You'd drive a man to it! I have a lot on my mind right now. I need cooperation, not a short fuse!"

"That's unfair! I didn't drive my husband away. He ran—as in after every skirt that swished by his desk! He's remarried and he was unfaithful to his second wife within six months of marrying her."

"Came back to familiar ground, did he?"

"Oh, that's low. But just what I'd expect of your type."

"What's my type?"

"Pompous, inconsiderate, vain."

Parnell wished he hadn't asked. "It's obvious you only look at the surface. I'm more than that."

"More of it, you mean. You can just consider us finished."

Parnell gaped. "Finished? What've we started?"

"Everything, and you know it!"

He backpedaled as fast as a frightened man could. "I haven't said anything. Have I said anything?"

Rebecca replied haughtily. "Body language speaks volumes." Her gaze tracked him to mid-thigh and stopped, a gesture that was allusive and unadorned.

Parnell got the message. His eyes went flat, like a cat's. His cheeks went hollow, the ridge of bones beneath his dark eyes appeared suddenly too prominent. "You felt me up when I was asleep."

The accusation rendered Rebecca speechless.

"Well c'mon," he egged, jaw thrusting. "Give it your best shot."

"You're gauche!"

"I don't know what that means."

"Low-down reprehensible worm!"

"Not bad," he mocked. "Not bad at all."

His tone seeped through Rebecca's frustration. Oh, he was a sly one. Well, she saw right through his ploy. He wanted sex. It was clear to her now. In the business of love, he was just as vulnerable as she. She looked him up and down and nodded. "I see right through you, Parnell."

He eyed her warily. She'd gone calm too quickly to suit him. She had a coy smile on her lips that made him stare at them, note how full they were, which made him think about kissing her.

"What does that mean?" he asked balefully, certain that somehow in the past few minutes he'd managed to shoot himself in the foot while his foot was in his mouth.

"Nothing," Rebecca replied airily and put her hand out to the fire.

Parnell pondered body language. His stomach began to ache. And anyway, he told himself, what did she know about men? She'd had a lush for a father and skirt chaser for a husband. She wouldn't know a good man if he fell into her lap. Saw through him! To hell in a basket. Just because there had been a bit of heraldic activity in his libido didn't mean anything. Considering the condition of his arse, he was lucky to have any! He was just about to tell her so when Jonesy burst out of the forest and tumbled down the snowy incline.

"Hey! Hey, Rebecca! Captain! We found a house!"

7

"WE'RE SAVED!" breathed Rebecca, stunned.

"Don't be too sure about that," Parnell warned in his rich careless voice. "We landed practically on their doorstep. You've noticed no one's come rushing out to greet us."

"Don't be so negative! Every time something good happens you knock it."

His eyebrows shot up. "What good happenings? You mean losing my plane? You mean taking a dip in ice water? Starving to death? Meeting you? Or maybe you mean 'good' as in putting up with the rowdy urchins you can't seem to control?"

Color deepened in Rebecca's cheeks. "You only think in terms of yourself—"

"That's not true. I'm responsible for—"

"A responsibility you'd rather not have—"

"There's no sin in that! I like—"

"I don't want to hear it!" She latched on to Nicholas and huffed her way up the incline where Santee waited and was urging them to hurry.

"I was just going to say I like a bit of peace and quiet," Parnell said soulfully into the empty air.

Molly tugged at his sleeve. "Will you carry me up the hill?"

"No. Stop hanging on me."

"If you don't, I'll start hollering and screaming. I'll tell Rebecca you hit me."

"Why you little twerp . . ." He watched her poky little face twisting, saw the intake of breath. "Don't you dare, you pint-sized witch!" He snatched her up. Grim-faced and thoughts black, he stalked after Rebecca with Molly riding happily on his shoulder.

The sight of him carrying Molly warmed Rebecca, dimmed her anger at him. "A house!" she cooed when he was in step beside her. "Oh, I hope they have coffee."

"I hope they can point me to the nearest road out of here."

In truth, he had no hope of that, much less coffee. It was possible, though, that he'd put the plane down in a national forest, which meant the house could be a ranger station of some sort; well-stocked with food, cots, blankets. Reasonably, it could be situated on a well-beaten path. If so, he could leave Rebecca and the kids while he hiked out. He might even meet the ground crew coming to rescue them. The rescue team could take over. They'd all be saved. He, in more ways than one. The thought cheered him immensely.

Santee, Jonesy and Yancy trudged eagerly ahead, retracing the footpath made in the snow. Rebecca judged the boys literally were leading them through dell and over hill. After a quarter mile she stopped to catch her breath. "How much farther?"

Santee pointed. "Just around that outcropping of rocks."

There was a scramble to be first around the ice-slick gray boulders. Rebecca skidded to a halt and gazed into the clearing.

Parnell lowered Molly to the path of beaten snow and came up behind Rebecca. "Well," he drawled, "I don't think you'll get a cup of coffee out of here." He surveyed the small dell in which stood a cabin that had long since seen its better days. Long since, he thought, like maybe a hundred years ago.

"The door's gone, and some of the roof," announced Jonesy excitedly. "But Santee and I figure we can fix it."

"I thought you said a house," Rebecca appealed, not wanting to believe in the dilapidated structure before her eyes, unwilling to give up hope of other people, food, immediate rescue.

"C'mon," Jonesy urged. "It's got a stove and bunks all around the walls and a bathroom even."

"An outhouse," Santee corrected.

"We're here, we might as well have a look," conceded Parnell.

Molly and Yancy, with Nicholas between them, raced to explore the new territory.

Rebecca's shoulders sagged as she watched the children run ahead. "I was so hoping..."

Parnell hesitated. She appeared unhappier than he felt. He knew it was a leader's responsibility to keep morale up. He wasn't certain of the best approach. After a moment's hesitation he put his arm around her. Her frown remained, but his own disposition improved at once. "We might find something we can use and who knows? Even from here the place looks sounder than the lean-to."

"Don't go getting cheerful," Rebecca touted, allowing him to propel her forward because she liked the feel of his arm across her shoulder. "I won't know what to make of it."

It impressed Parnell that she didn't make any effort to shrug him off. He tried not to read anything into it. That business down by the lake. She was beginning to like him. She had admitted it—in a vague way. In which case . . . in which case . . . he slewed away from the idea before it could make sense and brought his arm back to his own side like a shot. He wasn't about to improve her morale that much!

"An old trapper's cabin," he pronounced, his voice only a little thick as he began to reconnoiter. He pointed out the rusted remains of traps hanging from pegs on the wall behind the ancient wood-burning stove. The stove too had a layer of rust. Parnell tapped it. "Bet it took a half dozen mules to drag this thing in here."

Rebecca had not missed the sudden change in his decorum, the way he snatched his hand back. She had the presentiment that he had taken flight from a sense of some preordained mystic junction point, a line over which he'd decided he'd never cross. She recognized that there was an elemental force working on both of them. He was fighting it. Well he could battle it all by himself. Falling in love was hard enough— She caught the clarity of her thought and gasped.

How ludicrous.

No, it wasn't.

Yes, it was.

Imagine falling for a man about whom she knew so little and who by his own lights disliked women and children. She was being irrational because she was hungry and tired and scared. That was it. Yet . . . a very important part of her wanted it to happen.

Parnell touched her arm. "You're not listening to a word I'm saying," he said crossly. "I might as well be talking to a tree."

"I was dreaming of coffee."

"I told you not to get your hopes up."

"I won't ever again."

The tone of her voice put Parnell on alert. "Are we having two different conversations here?"

"Don't be silly," she said and began another inspection of the cabin.

In addition to the stove in the first room, a smaller second room had a stone-built fireplace. There were bunks on two walls. Built head to head. She tested one. It was still sturdy. Near the iron stove was a shelf of sorts on which stood an old wooden bucket, empty tin cans, a cast-iron pot, a fork with bent tines. A rough-hewn table with a leg missing leaned askew upon a planked floor ankle-deep in debris. Rebecca saw the cabin through her dismay. "It's a mess. And there's a smell."

"Want to look at the next house on our list then?"

"Very funny."

Parnell wrinkled his nose. "Probably some wild animal has used it as a lair." He looked up at the holes in the roof that could easily be covered by brush. "I agree with the boys. We ought to move in here. I wouldn't mind having a solid roof over my head tonight. The temperature's dropping. I can feel it." He tapped on a mud-chinked wall. "We'd have more protection from windchill."

"I wouldn't mind having some solid food," Jonesy said pointedly as he picked up and inspected bits of flotsam from the floor.

"Why move?" Rebecca balked. "We'll be out of here today, tomorrow at that latest. Where'll we get the energy to—"

Parnell shooed the kids outside. "Now look. We don't have any idea when an air or ground crew will show up. It might be today, it might be a week from today. We'd be better off here. Besides, in the event that I have to walk out of here to get help, I'd feel better knowing you had some protection from the weather."

"Walk out?" Rebecca swallowed on a suddenly dry throat. "You wouldn't. Not and leave us. Suppose you died of exposure? Or got hurt?"

"What do you care?" He told himself he only wanted to know out of curiosity.

She assayed his tone, the implication; her heart tripped.

She felt suddenly shy of Parnell, yet the very vulnerable side of her craved him, craved a strong man to protect her. Parnell had proved his strength and stamina time and again. She couldn't discount it. She now found him exciting and appealing and having substance beyond the surface. It did no good to attribute the thoughts to hunger or exhaustion. She and he were becoming united in more than the cause of survival. She wondered if he guessed.

"Care?" she replied evenly. "Of course I care—about all of us."

Parnell didn't like her answer. It was too generic. Perversely, he pushed for one more to his liking, one to soothe his vanity. "But earlier you said—"

"No I didn't."

"Yes, you did."

"You misunderstood."

"You're playing games with me."

"Surviving a plane crash and being lost in the wilderness is a game?"

"Now you sound combative. I don't understand you. We were getting along good."

"When?"

He looked at her through slitted lashes. "Have it your way. Just remember, I'm in charge."

"How can I not? You remind me with every other breath."

Parnell ignored the dripping sarcasm. "We're moving in here."

"Whatever you say."

"Good. I say swab the decks."

"Swab the who?"

"That's Navy lingo," he said snidely. "It means clean the place up. Make everything shipshape."

"You're insufferable. I'm more than a housekeeper, you know."

"Really? Like to prove it?" He dealt her a fraudulent grin that stretched to reveal strong teeth made whiter by contrast to his dark beard stubble.

She looked at him from beneath her lashes and disposed of his leer. "Why certainly, Captain Stillman. Right after high tea."

"Cripes. A guy can't even make a joke around you," he complained in an attempt to save face. "I'm the boss, see. I'm supposed to have the last word."

"Well, all right. Have it."

He couldn't think of one. Instead, he focused on her wide, full-lipped, unlipsticked mouth. It entered his mind that a man could go to heaven nibbling on her lower lip. It also entered his mind that either you got them, or you let them get you. He had the unhappy feeling he was on his way to being had. And he was hardly putting up a fight. Two females in the group, he thought, and both of them had out-maneuvered him. He made a derisive noise. "Never mind."

"Your problem is you think a woman ought to fall over at the knees every time you open your mouth."

"Boy, are you off the mark!" He turned away and yelled for Jonesy and Santee.

"Stop screaming at those kids."

"They're out of sight. What do you want me to do, whisper?"

"Don't bully."

"Next you'll be insisting I walk around on my tippy toes."

"You're hopeless," she said. Leaving him standing on the threshold she moved deeper into the cabin to see what could be salvaged.

Parnell slipped around to the side of the cabin and leaned against it a moment, in hopes of retrieving his mental bearings.

He had never been more nervous. He hadn't spent so much time in a woman's company since he couldn't remember when. It was telling on him. He was feeling things. Like protective. Like, maybe Rebecca needed him. He was thinking about have sex with her all the time now. He tried to shy away from the idea. His feet were cold. His bum hurt. Think about that. No, better not think on any area below the belt. It was all her fault. She should never have snuggled up to him last night and stuck her head under his chin. She did it on purpose.

Nicholas came around the corner and plowed into him.

"Hey! Watch where you're going."

"I can't."

Parnell winced. "Sorry."

"That's okay. I'm just getting the feel of the cabin. What side am I on?"

"East."

"Front door faces north then?"

"Right."

"Where's the bathroom?"

Parnell judged the distance. "Twenty-five paces downhill on the diagonal from the southeast corner."

Nicholas looked confused. "Tell me on the clock."

"Oh. From the corner of the cabin the outhouse is at eleven o'clock."

"Got it," Nicholas said.

Parnell took the child's arm. "C'mon, I'll take you."

The boy jerked away. "I can do it myself."

"Independent little bugger."

"Have to be," Nicholas said with brevity. He groped his way to the corner and began slowly counting off the steps. Parnell watched until he'd reached the outhouse and disappeared inside. Poor little sod, he thought with a bit of grudging admiration, wishing he could do something nice for the boy. Hell! Now even the kids were getting under his skin. No doubt in some sly way, Rebecca put them up to it.

He spied the older boys horsing around atop the boulders and whistled for them.

AS DARKNESS APPROACHED Rebecca wondered, not for the first time that day, how the pioneer women and settlers had managed day in and day out. It wasn't so much the loss of plumbing and electricity she missed, though she longed for a bath, it was the small everyday items one took so much for granted, like brooms, dustpans and toilet paper. She was improvising, but not without hard thought and some difficulty.

A small tree with a wealth of bare limbs had been made into a sweep to clear sixty years or more of spider webs, mice and bird nests from the chimney in the smaller room. A cheery fire burned now and the younger children sprawled drowsily in front of it. Santee was out with Parnell gathering more wood.

And they were going to need it. Little of the warmth from the fireplace penetrated into the room in which she worked. The temperature had continued to fall all afternoon and sullen clouds scudding out of the north had blocked out the sun. Parnell had forecast more snow. Already scattered flakes had begun to fall.

The busy work had a side effect in that it had kept them all from thinking of hunger. And of a rescue that had never come. For a moment Rebecca stood in the open doorway. Nearby was a pile of leafy cedar limbs set aside to fill up the opening once they were all in for the night. She enjoyed the fragrance of the freshly chopped wood, but the air chilled her ears and scalp and drove her back inside. At full dark Parnell and Santee returned.

"There's nothing like coming home to a snug house," said Parnell approvingly as he warmed his cold-reddened hands at the fire.

"We saw a deer," said Santee. "It came down to the lake to drink where we'd chopped a hole in the ice to put the wooden bucket to soak. The captain thinks he can get a shot at it if we build a blind."

"Kill a deer?" Rebecca said, not liking the idea. Putting the wooden bucket in the lake to swell the wood and make tight against its wooden straps had been Santee's suggestion. Rebecca did approve of that. And she was proud of Santee. He was proving himself as he'd never had the opportunity to do in the city. He needed a woodsman for a father, she thought. She'd put that in his file when they got back. When they got back. She found herself wondering, what if no one comes? Impossible. Someone has to come. But what if no one comes?

"He's stringy lookin'," said Parnell. "Probably an old bull that was turned out of his harem. And don't count on it. I'm a better pilot than I am a marksman."

Then the import of what Santee had said struck Rebecca. "You had to chop the ice? Is the lake frozen solid again?"

"On the surface. Not solid. But it's getting there. I think in a few more hours."

"But it's pitch black out there!"

"I've given some thought to that." If he broke through the ice and went under it . . . he didn't like the odds, but all of them were becoming lethargic from lack of food. The faces of the younger children were pinched, even in sleep, he thought, as he gazed at the two who were snoozing under Rebecca's coat upon the bunk nearest the fire. "We can build up a bonfire near the lake edge. That'll help guide me."

"You're certain you have food on the plane?" she asked, needing reassurance, aware of the fact that he was less confident of early rescue now and was planning for a longer duration.

"Positive," he replied trying to recall the list of rations. He'd glanced at them once before he'd deflated and stored the Air Force surplus A-3 raft. The labels on the food packets then had sounded dry and repulsive. "I remember malted milk tablets, powdered eggs, bacon paste, instant coffee—"

Rebecca's face lit up. "Instant coffee? Really?" In her sleep, Molly coughed. Rebecca went at once to feel the child's brow. "I think she's running a temperature." She moved Yancy to another bunk, lest whatever Molly might have was catching.

"Keep her warm and dry," Parnell offered. "Especially her feet," he added, thinking of his own. The cold and damp had crept through his boots. He was going to have to borrow his socks back from Rebecca to make the attempt to reach the plane tonight. Aching and trying not to show it, he sat down in front of the fire. He wished now that he'd let Rebecca medicate his arse that morning. It was prickly as heck again, shooting pain up his spine. Just thinking of her hands touching him caused a pleasant shiver; an antidote to the pain.

Rebecca urged the older boys, not without some argument, to lie down on the bunks and rest. Santee balked until she assured him she'd wake him when it came time to hike down to the lake. For a while she sat in the shadow of Molly's bunk, listening to the girl breathe.

Once all the children were asleep, the cabin offered more privacy than Rebecca anticipated.

Alight by the glow of the fire, Parnell seemed an island to himself and very much alone. His movements were stiff as he bent to unlace his boots. He was in pain. She could tell. She couldn't bear it that he hurt.

That decided it. She settled the matter in her mind's eye. Settled it in her heart where her realistic dreams and aspirations lay. She was falling in love with an unkempt, cynical, nettlesome rogue who was still hung up on the ache of old wounds from a long-past failed marriage.

But then, if she suddenly became sweet and lovable, he'd confront her with a dense intractable funk as he had earlier. Her only course was to keep an acid tongue until he was caught beyond defense. But not too acid. He was bound to have weak moments during which the right words, the right kind of gesture would not go amiss.

And one of those moments was now.

She glided quietly to him and knelt down. "Let me help you."

Parnell, tired to the bone, acquiesced. "Might not be a pleasant sight," he warned.

"I know. I made the boys dry out their shoes and socks this afternoon. Their feet were wrinkled from wet snow." Parnell's feet, without the protection of his woolen socks, were far worse; frozen and bloodless. Rebecca swallowed back a lump in her throat. "You should've said something! Damn you! You don't have to be brave on my account." She took the T-shirt that now served as washcloth, rinsed it in the cast-iron pot of warm water and began to wash, then massage his feet.

"This is embarrassing," Parnell told her; it was almost Biblical. On the other hand, he found it highly erotic.

When feeling began to surge back into his numbed limbs an involuntary groan escaped him. Rebecca glanced sharply at him, then softened her expression, deciding she needed to use every wile she possessed to get inside him. Her hand moved above his ankles to his calves.

"Better?" she asked.

He sighed. "Truly, that feels wonderful." Her fingers were magical. There was a tingling throughout his body. His heart thundered. But he couldn't accustom himself to the sudden excess of emotion. "Maybe you ought to stop," he said, voice thick.

"Why don't you take off your jacket and lie down on it?"

"Then what?" He gazed at her with a varlet's eye of suspicion.

"I'll massage your back and neck. You have to be sore from sleeping on brush. I was," she added to make her suggestion appear ordinary and plausible. She wished to touch him all over; an impractical wish at the moment with all the children sleeping nearby.

"Why do you want to do that for me?" No one had ever paid him such intimate attention.

"Oh," she replied, presenting an arabesque of indifference. "To pass the time, to keep my mind off of how hungry I am."

Parnell told himself he would get up later feeling unaffected, feeling right and sane. He lay down on the sheepskin lining. But when Rebecca's cool hands slid under his shirt to knead his flesh, all he felt was short of breath and giddy.

He bit down on his tongue to keep from emitting exclamations of pleasure. Rebecca leaned so near his ear that he felt her warm breath. The giddiness increased. "Do relax," she urged in a whisper.

Not in a thousand years, Parnell thought. Not with this coming down on him. His response to her was visceral. Lust, not love. A familiar panic rose in him. He knew all about love and loving. It left you open for rejection, not to mention domination. And the more you loved somebody, the more those things hurt. Damn! What was she doing? Kissing his ear it felt like. Goose bumps erupted along his arms. "Hey!" he crooned, fighting the quaver in his voice. "Stop . . . that."

To Rebecca his protest sounded as if he were begging her to continue. Her tongue darted in his ear. "You don't like—"

"I do, but—" He was breathing heavily.

"But what?" she asked, and trailed her fingertips down his spine. He shivered.

"I'm getting excited. That's as nice a way I can think to put it. A certain part of me is about to explode."

"I don't mind," Rebecca said, driven by the desire to experience the full gamut of feelings that went with having the man she wanted wanting her.

Parnell twisted slightly out of her reach. Firelight tinged her flushed complexion a burnt sienna, her hair was in a tangle. It made her appear exotic and lush. He glanced quickly about the cabin. Every last one of the barbarians was soundly asleep. Just when he'd welcome an interruption, an argument or fisticuffs. Undependable little beasts.

"Listen," he said, "I don't think what you propose is ethical. Under the circumstances, I mean."

"I'm not proposing anything," returned Rebecca innocently. Retreating somewhat, she wound her arms about her legs and rested her chin on her knees. "You felt good. I got carried away for a moment—"

Parnell's skepticism knew no bounds. "In my book what you just did is called foreplay. Sexual foreplay."

A telltale blush colored Rebecca's cheeks. She had to rein in. "You misunderstood."

"Signals like that I don't misunderstand."

It was bluff or bait. She baited. "You must admit, you're a fine figure of a man. I imagine you get a lot of attention and flattery."

He never got any. He shrugged. "Sometimes. When I get away from the airport." Which was seldom. Or when he shaved and revealed his dimples, a thing he wasn't inclined to do until his beard got itchy. He looked at her soberly. "You weren't flirting with me?"

"No. Oh, no. I didn't mean to. I was admiring you."

His ego caught and flared. "Well, that's all right, then." He felt a sudden obligation to return the compliment. "You're not bad looking yourself."

Rebecca lowered her lashes, her smile, a mixture of seduction and reticence. "Thank you." She stretched, arms high, back arched; a shamefully provocative display of herself. And she knew it. But in the past she'd overthought scores of decisions, missing opportunities. Parnell was the man for her. No wiffle-waffling about it. Therefore it followed, didn't it? He had to fall in love with her. That meant she'd have to make a lasting impression upon him. Very lasting, so lasting that once they'd returned to Boise, his impressions of her would intensify, not wane. "We'd better get some rest, don't you think?" She lowered her arms and began to remove her boots.

Parnell was reluctant to agree. She might want to lie down next to him. He wouldn't be able to keep himself under control after the way she kept flaunting herself.

"You're not thinking about taking off your clothes...?" he blurted.

"What's wrong with you? I'm just going to dry your socks! You'll need them out on the lake. I have some knee-high nylons I can wear instead." There were iron hooks embedded in the mud mortar between the stones of the fireplace, she hung the socks on them.

"I'll just stay here by the fire and snooze," he said, fishing for where she meant to sleep.

"I'll bunk down with Molly, make sure she stays warm. You'll wake me when it's time to try the ice?"

"Right."

Rebecca got as comfortable as the hard slats allowed. She'd done it, she thought. She'd been more forward and brazen than she'd believed possible. She had Parnell's attention now. She was certain of that.

But was it a forever kind of thing? she wondered. She was under pressure and people who were under pressure did crazy things. As for all their fussing back and forth—well, when one is scared, as she was, one took that fear out on whomever was around. Parnell was around. Eyes shuttered, thoughts growing vague, she watched him at the hearth until at last she slept, disturbed only by the rumblings of her empty stomach.

LYING ON HIS SIDE in front of the fire with his head resting on his bent elbow, Parnell's mind was busy looking for a reasonable explanation for Rebecca's behavior. She could deny it into the hereafter, he thought, but she must've felt him up while he slept last night. Must've!

He couldn't figure anything else for the sly change in her attitude toward him.

He knew one thing as fact: women were the strangest creatures God had a hand in making. One minute they hated you and the next . . . He caught his breath. He wouldn't consider that even if she hired a skywriter to tell the world!

Just to indulge himself, he closed his eyes and tried to imagine what his life might be like with a woman as comely as Rebecca at his side. No mental picture materialized. The idea was so foreign, so beyond the realm of possibility, so frightening, his mind stayed blank.

He'd have to watch what went on, he decided. He'd handle it with a bit of himself, but he'd keep the rest of himself in reserve. Any woman who took his attentions to her as something more than a willingness to pass a short time pleasurably had another think coming.

Including and most especially, Rebecca Hollis!

8

IT HAD BEGUN TO SNOW in earnest and there was no moon. Parnell walked ahead, bent low into the wind, and Rebecca could only just see the outline of his figure against the snow. Santee brought up the rear. Rebecca measured her steps. She was weary and weak from hunger. The deep winter darkness enclosed them. It was an eerie feeling. She shivered as much from the odd sensation as from the cold. She guessed the temperature was well below zero.

At the lake's edge Parnell stirred the embers of the fire and after some coaxing, brought it to life. The wind blew away its warmth. Rebecca beat her arms and stamped her feet to keep warm, but again, the howling wind blew away any warmth she managed to work up. "I'm freezing!"

"I warned you," Parnell said. "Go back to the cabin."

"I'm staying."

"You don't have to be gutsy to the point of death, you know."

"I couldn't bear the suspense—waiting in the cabin. The not knowing if you made it or if you didn't."

He pulled her closer to the fire. "I just might get used to you worrying about me."

His nearness reminded her of what her healthy body yearned for. She smiled and shook her head. Parnell moved off to inspect the ice.

Santee took the wooden bucket from the lake. In the firelight, he examined it, pronouncing it free of leaks. "Now we can haul water from the lake instead of melting snow."

"That's good, Santee. You've really come into your own. I don't think we could've made it this long without you and your smart thinking."

"The captain's pretty smart—"

"It was your idea to soak the bucket. He said to burn it."

"I just read about it somewhere," he mumbled.

"I guess I'll try it," Parnell said.

"I'll go with you," Rebecca said.

"Like hell. Suppose the ice doesn't hold?"

"Two have a better chance. We'd have each other's help."

"Yes, but if we were both drowned, the kids couldn't make it alone." He glanced at the SOS. It had lost its luminosity. Snow flurries were beginning to dim the orange-painted troughs.

"Let's wait until daylight. A few more hours of being hungry won't hurt. We're getting used to it."

"There's a blizzard coming, Rebecca. Look at the way that wind's gusting. It's picked up a few knots just since we've gotten down here." He suspected a few more hours without food would weaken him beyond measure. The warmed water they'd been drinking offered no sustenance from which his body could draw energy. It'd been more than three days since he'd had a hot meal. He turned his collar up. "I'm going."

"Wait!" Rebecca insisted.

"For what?"

She reached up and hugged his neck, buried her face in his chest. "Good luck. Be careful."

He held her tightly for a moment, thinking how nice it was to have someone worry about him. "I'll be fine. Look, if the lake's frozen all the way out to the plane we're only talking about twenty minutes. No need to make a big deal out of it."

Rebecca and Santee followed him a few feet onto the ice. Parnell, gesturing with the hand axe, made them turn back. The wind sang, the snowfall thickened, visibility dropped to a few yards. He was soon out of sight. Rebecca and Santee were soon forced to move from the ice and hunker down by the fire on the embankment.

Snow swirled and piled up around them. The fire hissed. More and more snow fell, blowing into their eyes and ears and down their necks. In half an hour they were both shaking with cold, teeth rattling.

"Oh, why doesn't he come back?" Rebecca wailed.

"We need two fires," Santee said, teeth chattering. "We can sit between them."

It wasn't the cold so much that slowed the building of the second fire, but hunger. She imagined she could feel the blood slowing in her veins. She crawled around on all fours gathering the wood, dragging it back for the second fire. *If I can barely move,* she thought miserably, *how must it be with Parnell?*

PARNELL WAS ELATED. The ice was holding.

The jutting nose of the plane had long since been covered with ice and snow. White against white, it had no definitive shape. When the wind whipped up snow flurries and tossed them about the frozen surface of the lake, the plane became almost invisible. He stumbled over the wingtip, which led him to the plane's bulk.

A vague smell greeted him as he stepped inside, but his brain didn't go so far as to identify it. He was preoccupied with trying to discern shapes in the pitch-black of the plane's interior. Wishing he had a flashlight, he moaned.

The emergency generator! He felt his way into the cockpit, found the switch with numbed fingers on the control panel. The lights came on. He sat in the pilot's seat for a moment. It was like coming home. He tried the radio. Nothing. The lights flickered, dimmed. He moved quickly to reconnoiter the cargo hold.

On the row of passenger seats he saw the thermos, a pair of gloves . . . He marked them for retrieval on his way out.

The view of the cargo made him sag. Mail carts were piled atop one another. The ones on the bottom were locked solidly into ice. The same water that had frozen to allow him safe passage was also frozen inside the plane. He could just make out the top portion of the locker where he'd stored the raft. Straining, he pulled several carts from atop one another, lined them up and crawled on top of them, going as deep into the rear of the plane as he could.

The wind battered the downed plane and whistled through the interior, the frame creaked. The lights flickered again. He held his breath. They stayed on. He wedged himself close to the walls and peered down. The bottom half of the locker door was blocked by submerged mail carts that were frozen into place. It'd take hours to hack through the ice to dislodge the carts and free the door. He shook his head. Outside the storm was increasing in intensity. Time was of the essence now, for Rebecca and Santee were exposed to the elements.

Quickly he rummaged through the twin overhead lockers. The first gave up his navy flight bag, two rolls of toilet paper, a stack of one-ounce bars of lavatory soap; the second, a jar of salt tables, a grease gun, a screwdriver. No food. But he had a change of clothing and his own toothbrush in the flight bag. The glum thought came that if he starved or froze to death, at least he could be buried clean. He shoved everything into the bag and crawled back the way he'd come.

He switched off the emergency generator and was debating whether or not to close and latch the door when his brain recognized the smell.

HE REACHED OUT and tugged at Rebecca's arm. There was no response. He tugged again and she didn't move. "Rebecca!" he yelled, shaking her.

She hardly stirred, but mumbled something he could not hear for the wind. Parnell went on shaking and yelling until Rebecca woke up, angry.

"Leave me alone. Leave me alone."

"What're you trying to do? Kill yourself? Get up!"

"I'm sleepy," she insisted.

"You should never have given in to the temptation to sleep!"

Santee had been more easily aroused, perhaps because of his youth, or excitement that kept adrenaline pouring into his system. Parnell turned on him. "You were supposed to keep each other awake, keep the fire going." He kicked at the embers. Sparks flew, then scattered in the face of the blizzard.

"We didn't mean to sleep. We were just trying to keep warm."

Parnell found his heart pounding in panic. If Rebecca died... The thought wasn't one he cared to dwell on. He brushed snow from her face, her hair, then dragged her, protesting, to her feet.

"I'm terribly hungry," she said, slurring her words.

"I know. I'll help you walk." He put an arm around her, lifted his flight bag with the other. "Santee, you take that box."

Uphill and against the wind, progress was slow. They kept sliding back. Parnell drew upon language like the Navy wordsmith he was. The growled epithets had an effect on Rebecca. She moved her feet. In the shelter of the forest, drifts piled up against rocks and trees. Parnell lost the path. Half-carrying, half-dragging Rebecca, he crashed through undergrowth. It took most of an hour to locate the cabin. Santee collapsed at the base of the great gray boulders in the clearing. After Parnell placed Rebecca on the hearth and shoved new wood on the fire, he went back for the boy.

Stumbling blindly he made a second trip for the box, then forced himself to take time to pull the branches back over the opening. He knew the blizzard would soon pile snow against them and seal the cabin off from the world.

REBECCA WOKE UP with a start. "What's wrong?" she called out.

Molly bent over and whispered into her ear. "The captain's mad. He's trying to fix the stove. I want to sit next to you."

"Mad?" Not yet alert, Rebecca coughed and dragged herself to a sitting position. "Mad at who?"

Parnell materialized before her. His face and beard were streaked with soot. "I see you decided to join us," he said with mournful sarcasm.

Rebecca took note of his tone. It all came rushing back. The storm, the vigil at the lake. "Oh! I must've—"

"Must've, my foot! You went to sleep in the face of a blizzard. You have about as much sense as a flea's tit. I thought you were dead."

"Santee?"

"He's fine. I'm the one who's not fine. I'm the one who's been baby-sitting! I'm— Don't tell me. You're gonna start crying again." He knelt down in front of her. "I could throttle you! You scared the hell out of me."

Molly scampered away. Whatever room the captain was in was not the room for her.

Rebecca said slowly, "Parnell . . ."

"Don't make eyes at me."

She sat unmoving, letting his full gaze rest upon her, then she reached out and lay her hand on his chest. "I'm sorry."

"You should be. The elements are nothing to fool around with. For the kids' sake, if you want to pretend this is a picnic outing or an adventure—okay. But the dangers are real. One careless move and we could freeze, starve, get hurt. When you're up against what we're up against, you don't get second chances. Don't forget it."

"I won't, not again."

"Hell!" he said and moved away before he did something disastrous, like take her into his arms and smother her with kisses.

Rebecca thought it was a good thing he moved away. She was about to throw herself at him. After a moment she said, "Did you get the rations?"

"No, but I found some apples. Somebody was shipping a crate to a sailor stationed on Guam." Christmas apples, the letter accompanying the crate had said, picked from the sailor's favorite tree. The one he'd fallen from and broken his arm when he was seven. The letter was signed 'Love, Mother.' Shipping fresh fruit was against postal regulations so he didn't feel too badly about confiscating the parcel. "We've eaten two apiece. I thought that was enough for the time being."

Rebecca's mouth watered. "No!" Then she sniffed, and because she couldn't keep from it, began to sob quietly.

Parnell sagged. "Damn! I knew it."

He went to the iron pot at the fire and withdrew the thermos where he'd stashed it to defrost.

"If apples make you whine, no telling the flood this'll bring."

He handed her a precious cupful of the coffee.

"Oh!" Rebecca's hands trembled as she sipped.

Yancy brought her two apples. Rebecca hugged him tightly, which had the effect of sending him scurrying back into the other room.

"Eat slowly," Parnell warned when she'd finished, suggested a third. Rebecca refused it.

"If two is all you ate—" She refilled the thermos cup. "I feel I've just dined at a banquet." She was almost to the point of crying again. When she was certain her voice was stronger, she said "You saved my life. All of our lives, again."

"I was saving my own neck, too." But he would never forget that sinking, stabbing feeling he had felt when, arriving back at the lake's edge, he had found her circled into a ball, asleep—nearly frozen. Another thirty minutes and she would've been lost to him forever. Had he stayed in the plane to chop through to the locker... For some few seconds a surge of emotion raged through him. It must be more than sex, he thought. Maybe it was love. But he didn't see how it could've crept up on him without him noticing. Anyway, they were strangers. Thrown together by happenstance. When they got out of this, she'd go her way, he'd go his. He'd be a fool to consider a woman like her doing otherwise.

Suddenly very formal, he said, "I was getting that old stove going, I'd better finish it. As for saving your life. We're even now."

Rebecca puzzled over his sudden coolness. Reluctantly, she let him go.

THE STORM RAGED for three days. The wind sang around the corners of the cabin, the noise becoming a constant.

To Rebecca's dismay, Parnell continued to maintain his distance. For hours on end she was pressed into thinking *What have I said? What have I done?* When she wearied of guessing, she tried to engage him in conversation. Beyond extreme politeness, he had nothing to say, nothing to volunteer.

During the times the blizzard seemed to lessen, he alone gathered wood out of the forest.

Excursions to the outhouse were sheer torture. The children were all for an indoor chamber pot. Rebecca refused on the grounds that some privacy and a modicum of modesty should be maintained.

The water well on the woodburning stove was filled with snow to melt. To make a hot meal, Rebecca boiled apples into sauce. They ate it, dipping into the iron pot with the thermos lid and the old tins and a chipped enamel plate.

She passed the time rooting in her suitcase and all the totes, setting aside items they could make use of.

It took more hours than she dreamed possible to keep the children and herself as clean and neat as circumstances allowed. The bars of soap Parnell had discovered were a godsend.

The boys plagued Parnell for tales of flying. At first he only told them skimpy stories, but one thing led to another and he found himself regaling them with how a plane is catapulted off a carrier, the dangers of flying into a hurricane . . . Soon he saw hero worship glowing in their eyes. He had never been worshiped before and found it a most gratifying experience. It almost put him in a good mood.

Once Rebecca caught him surreptitiously staring at her. She tried to approach him, but as if she were a blot on his well-ordered life or as if he were in a panic—Rebecca suspected panic—he moved off the bunk and went to help Santee. With the screwdriver and grease gun the boy was trying to rework one of the old rusted traps.

Each time she even looked as if she meant to speak to Parnell he found something that needed doing that took him from her presence. Snow had to be knocked

off the roof lest the rotten timbers fall in; over her pro-
tests he replaced the brush pile with the door from the
outhouse; snow had to be hauled in to melt for water.
He was so polite and correct there was no doubt his was
purposeful behavior.

She dallied with her cosmetics, considered applying
some but thought that might be too obvious a ploy to
garner his attention. She was as enthralled with his
stories as the children. When one of them raised a
question, he answered it. When she did the same, he
raved, ranted and sulked to the extent that she'd been
obliged to make the noble gesture of keeping her mouth
shut lest he go mute and deprive the children.

On the third night of the storm, the wind died and
the sudden silence woke her. As always, she listened for
a moment to Molly's breathing. She'd been doling out
the aspirins to the child in halves. Now Molly sounded
fine. Rebecca sat up on the side of the bunk. No one else
had awakened. The four boys shared two bunks to
leave one free for Parnell. She glanced at him. In the
light from the fiery embers she could only make out that
he slept with his elbow crooked over his eyes.

Because it seemed the thing to do, because it created
a semblance of normalcy, she had insisted that everyone sleep in their pajamas. Coats were used as blankets. In spite of the primitive conditions, the cabin was
"home."

She shoved her feet into her slippers and glided across
the room to add a small log to the fire. She then went
to do the same in the front room. Keeping the fires going
had proved the most arduous of tasks, second only to
attempts at keeping the kids clean. They were surviving in a civilized manner—but only just.

She returned to the hearth and sat down, hugging her legs, chin resting on her knees and wondered if the outside world had given them up for dead. Please, she prayed, let them keep looking.

She felt a twinge of hunger, but took her restless mind elsewhere. Be grateful for this bit of peacefulness, she told herself. Enjoy the privacy...privacy! She had been longing for a good wash.

PARNELL WAS WIDE AWAKE. Curious about Rebecca moving about in the middle of the night, he adjusted his elbow so that he could watch her.

He no longer used her nightgown as a pillow; she was wearing it. But the scent of the gown stayed with him, filled his head. Wanting somebody so bad it hurt was something else, he thought. Having to keep up the pretense that he didn't want her was driving him crazy. Not only that, he was having a dreadful time making his genitals behave. It kept seeping into his brain that he was in love with her. Real love. He held his breath and struggled with that utterly paralyzing thought as he watched her poke around in her suitcase.

She took up something, tucked it under one arm, then using the hem of her nightgown, removed the iron pot from the hearth and disappeared into the other room. He'd gotten a glimpse of her legs when she raised the gown. Very nice legs made copper-colored by the firelight.

After a few moments he heard water splashing. He'd just see what she was up to. He wouldn't speak to her. She might misunderstand, think he was suggesting something, seeking her out for reasons other than simple curiosity.

The firebox door on the old stove was open, throwing off a feeble, flickering light. In that light Rebecca stood, naked. She was pouring water over herself. Dipping it can by tin can out of the iron pot, reaching above her head, letting the water sluice over her body. Parnell inhaled deeply and held his breath.

Her name escaped his lips.

She did not turn around, but her heart began to beat hard in her chest. She could feel it hammering, and feel the rise and fall of her breasts. "I'm bathing," she said.

"Yes, I heard you."

She hoped he'd approach her, and told herself hope was pointless. But now... "I didn't mean to wake you." Her voice was tremulous. She dropped the can into the iron pot, moved to reach for the gown that she'd hung on a wall peg. Her fingers poised there she waited for some sign that Parnell wanted her. Loved her.

His need for her grew, becoming more savage and immediate. "You didn't wake me. I couldn't sleep."

"Oh." Rebecca felt deflated. Her fingers closed over to gown.

"You're beautiful." It wasn't what he wanted to say. It sounded lame, but flowery words didn't come easy to him. Curiosity and courage meshed. His muscles were quivering with tension. The pressure building inside him had to be released. Either he must do what his entire being demanded or leave the cabin. Without warning he closed the distance between them, placed his hand over hers. "Don't cover yourself."

All at once the tension between them was a tangible thing. She was aware of a stillness of emotion, as if all thoughts, sensations were in abeyance, locked in the eye of a storm, a lull before another onslaught. If not that, whatever it was had a physical presence of its own, stronger than her own will. The puddle of water she stood in began to cool; she hardly noticed. She didn't speak, but touched his face with the tips of her fingers. His lips were taut and cool, the tactile contact with his beard—much more than stubble now—gave her a tingle of pleasure.

Parnell lifted his hand and touched her damp hair. "I want you very much. I've wanted you for a long time. Unless you go back in the other room right now, it's going to happen."

Rebecca didn't move. Go! she told herself.

The seconds went by, marked only by their strained breathing. When at last she felt Parnell pull her body against his own, she was ready to yield. Her breasts trembled and the nipples were swollen and hard.

"A moment," he whispered and went into the other room, returning with an armload of clothing. He spread his coat on the floor near the side of the stove and led her to it, then he quietly closed the firebox.

"Perhaps we . . ." Rebecca whispered. She was having second thoughts. "Suppose one of the children wakes?"

He stretched out his hand and touched her cheek. "They're sound asleep. I checked." He removed his clothes and layered them with the others he'd brought. "Tuck these around you. I don't want you cold."

Rebecca almost laughed, caught herself in time. "I'm not cold. I'm not at all cold." The degree of her desire was frightening. She wanted to talk, perhaps lessen it, but was conscious of the silent sleeping cabin that prevented voice above a whisper. Sex! she thought. It was taking her over, running her body, dictating to her. Oh! She wanted it to be so much more than that.

At first he only put his arm across her; their bodies touched. That was all. It was the only important thing. Slowly he drew his tongue along her lips. He bulged hot and tumescent against her thigh and she thought of tasting him, but not yet, not now. Such sensitivities were no part of this particular moment. Then his strong sure hands began to explore her, know her.

They had both lost every vestige of fat. Rebecca thought herself too thin. He cupped her breasts with his hands, she felt a surge of pure pleasure and her concern about thinness faded.

The bits and pieces of fabric bunched beneath her, a soft pallet. There was a building frenzy in her loins. She had been married yet she had never been touched so, never been made to feel as if she could sense the blood coursing through her veins and pumping life into her heart.

He spread apart her flesh and entered her, the penetration slow and purposeful as if he were only now arriving at some shrine at which he meant to worship.

Her hips rose, straining to take him completely inside her, and she rose and fell to his rhythm. She could feel him swelling within her, filling a hollow depth; could sense the ending coming upon her much too soon. She was held in his grip, powerless to halt her movements, or his.

Outside a sudden wind gusted. It had the sound of a roaring cataract far away. Then Rebecca realized the roar was inside her head, pulsating. His beard brushed her cheek.

"Parnell . . ." she said between gasps.

He increased his tempo. The breaking, tidal release closed over them both in great looping gusts.

THE STRAIN OF FINDING himself in love was too much for Parnell. He looked for a way to shake it off, disavow it. "You seduced me," he accused.

He sounded so lachrymose Rebecca realized it was going to take him some time to come to grips with his emotions. He was arguing against Destiny. He'd have to find out for himself that warring against Fate was a losing battle.

She said, "Funny isn't it? How you're only now complaining?" Despite his gloom he had not yet loosened his hold on her. The room was becoming cool. She felt a draft whip across her feet.

"We can't let this go one bit further. You might as well know. I'm a coward."

She laughed. "There are cowards and there are cowards."

"I'm not good at word games either. All I know how to do is fly."

"You sure had me soaring."

"I did?" He tripped over his ego. "I mean, so what?"

"So, nothing. We don't have to do this ever again." Her hand rested on his chest. She let it slide down his abdomen, drawing her fingertips down and up the inside of his thigh.

His voice thickened. "Well, that's all right then."

"Besides, it was just a fluke, wouldn't you say? We're adults. I guess the strain of being lost, hungry and in each other's company for days on end got to us." He shifted his hips as if to make himself more comfortable. Her fingertips brushed his growing erection. In the dark, Rebecca smiled. "I'd better finish rinsing my hair. If there's anything I hate, it's shampoo-sticky hair."

Before he could do more than issue a low groan, she moved off the pallet, opened the firebin door to the stove and added a stick of wood.

Parnell sat up. His enlarged shaft ached for what her caressing hand had promised. He wanted her again. But how could he admit that now, damn it!

"There's plenty of warm water left if you want to bathe," Rebecca told him as she pulled her night gown over her head. "You'll have to stand over here though. There's a crack in the floor where the water runs out." She retrieved a shirt from the pallet makings and began to dry her hair.

"You're teasing me," Parnell said. He couldn't seem to control the thing between his legs. He felt it waving like an unstrung flagpole.

"I'm not. I'm just respecting your wishes."

"I hate women who do that."

"Oh. Well, what would you have me do?"

"Nothing." It was too monstrous an idea to change his stand. Let a woman find a man's weak point and the rest of his life she'd make a man miserable. Wheedling this and that until she got her way on everything.

The sticks Rebecca had put in the stove caught and flared. In the sudden spark of light she glimpsed the engorged length of him. She had thought to use a woman's subterfuge, to go back to her cot, leaving him with an ache that would keep her in his mind. She couldn't make herself do it. She knelt down on the pallet before him. "Would you like for me to sit on that for a minute?" she asked softly, reaching for him.

The words were feathers that raced down his back-bone and lodged firmly between his legs. "You're se-ducing me again," he moaned, trying to keep the delight out of his voice.

Rebecca took a deep breath. "It'll be the last time," she whispered. "I promise." She positioned herself as she guided him fully inside her.

He was conscious of her weight, felt her pelvic mus-cles contract. A band of tenderness encircled his chest and tightened on his heart.

"That's...all...right...then..." he said and be-gan to knead her buttocks. Rebecca moved and found her rhythm.

He was helpless against the crazy way his heart was acting now. He was sure it was affecting his brain, the way he saw things. But tomorrow he was going to purify himself of certain impulses. Then he'd be straight again. Normal.

Rebecca leaned forward and nibbled on his earlobe. His thoughts faded.

Something stronger prevailed.

9

REBECCA STARTED to say something, but Parnell wouldn't let her.

"Just keep unloading those mail carts," he said, turning away to continue hacking at the ice-bound locker. The sound of the hatchet cracking ice reverberated throughout the plane and echoed the breadth and width of the frozen lake.

"That noise hurts my ears," bewailed Molly. "I wanna go make a snowman."

Rebecca acquiesced, and watched the child scamper as freely as her heavy shoes allowed across the frozen lake to shore.

Wind had swept the surface clean of powdery snow, the ice gleamed with an iridescent sheen of sunlight being fed through a prism. Landward it was much different. The drifts were high and almost impossible to negotiate.

The younger boys were making a game of scooping snow from the SOS. Santee had begged permission from Parnell and was in the forest setting the two traps he'd managed to reclaim from rust.

The contrast between the boys' laughter on the shore and Parnell's mood was obvious. No wonder Molly wanted to escape. Inside the plane was about as cheerful as a morgue.

From the moment they'd awakened and faced each other, Parnell had worn the look of a man who'd suffered a great injustice and couldn't figure out who to blame for his misery.

The Morning After Syndrome, Rebecca thought. Women suffered it, but it surprised her to think men did. Especially Parnell. Maybe there was something to the suggestion that the American male was the Great Pretender of the twentieth century!

Watching him swing the hatchet gave her insight into why his clothes seemed to misfit him so. He worked with his entire body. His sweater had ridden up, his shirttail escaped his belt, his cuffs, neatly rolled earlier, now drooped.

The poor darling, Rebecca thought. His face drooped, too. He had dark circles under his eyes.

He straightened a moment to release tension from his cramped muscles and out of the corner of his eye saw the hint of laughter about her mouth. "What're you smiling at?" he said, glaring at her.

"I'm happy. I feel wonderful. Don't you?"

Parnell thought, *She's gloating.* She had her claws into him, but good!

Last night after she'd gone back to the bunk she shared with Molly, he'd gotten up and actually teetered, his legs were so weakened from lovemaking. He'd splashed water on himself, called it bathing and worried the night away on thoughts that she'd wormed her way into his psyche so that he couldn't do without her. The idea had clung to his brain like a bloodthirsty leech. He'd spent hours envisioning her living with him in the house trailer behind the hangar. Most of the daydream had taken place in the bedroom. And somehow without him even saying it, she knew. She was evidently plumbing new ways to make him miserable.

"You're supposed to be salvaging the mail, not standing around grinning."

"Right." She kept on smiling. "What if nobody comes back to get it?"

"You don't know postal inspectors. If it's got a stamp on it, they'll get it."

Rebecca glanced at the packages stacked in the cockpit and along the walls above the frozen water line. "You think there might be other foodstuffs in any of those?"

"If we run out of food again, we'll look." He needed to get away from her, get his thoughts clear. "I want to tell you something. I'm hiking out of here as soon as I can."

"No!"

"I am."

"You can't leave us to fend for ourselves!"

"I'm going after help. We've been here six days. No, seven. Don't you understand? They've stopped looking. They wouldn't expect that we've been able to survive the storm we just had. They probably don't even consider we survived the crash."

"But you said—"

"Now I'm saying different."

"It's me you're running from. It's me you want to escape."

Parnell couldn't form the words to deny the truth of that. Rebecca seemed like almost a part of him now. Yet it was irrational to believe their relationship would go on once back in Boise. If he got in deeper, he'd just be setting himself up for heartache. "I'll make sure you have plenty of food and wood before I go."

"With plenty of food and wood we could last here indefinitely! All of us."

"I have an air freight business going to pot, Rebecca. We're prisoners here, not pioneers. There's a difference."

"The difference is that you made love to me. Now you wish you hadn't!"

"I got carried away. If you hadn't pranced around naked, it wouldn't have happened. But this morning I remembered why I don't like you. Loving a woman wrecks a man."

She didn't know whether to laugh or cry. "You were a wreck when I met you. You still are. I can't see that making love has improved you any."

The sinews at the side of his neck moved slightly, tightening. His narrowed, unsmiling eyes bore down on her. "It hasn't. But I see that look in your eye. You're figuring ways to make me over. You're not gonna get the chance."

"As it happens I like you just the way you are."

"I've heard that tale before."

"I'm in love with you." He went pale so suddenly, Rebecca knew she'd crossed a boundary he wasn't yet ready to recognize. She hurried on. "However, that's not your problem, it's mine. I'll deal with it. The psychologists will probably come up with a very good explanation. We were thrown together by unusual circumstances, cramped quarters, lack of privacy.... But I'm warning you, I'm not some little annoyance you're going to be able to forget."

His stomach knotted. "It was lust, plain and simple. You ever heard of lust?"

"Call it by any name you like—sexual static, lust, whatever. We both enjoyed it."

"I got ice to chop." He went to do it. He wasn't about to give her an open hold on him. She had it. But what she didn't know was better for him. After he'd positioned himself he glanced back at her. She appeared more disconsolate than he felt. "If you start crying," he yelled, "so help me, I'll throttle you!"

"Why should I cry? I don't have anything to cry about. Unless being lost in the wilderness with a horse's ass qualifies. I'm going to check on the kids."

Parnell stared unseeing at the ice-encrusted locker. There it was. She didn't really love him. He could tell. She was calling him names. "People in love don't fuss and fight," he bellowed.

Hearing his outburst, Rebecca stepped back inside the plane. "How old are you, Parnell?"

"Forty-two."

"Incredible," she said.

There was a look of knowing instinct and intuition on her face. Parnell felt his palms dampen. He sensed he'd somehow just destroyed his own defenses. But he couldn't fathom how. He took the whiskey flask from his back pocket and downed a long draught. "See," he muttered, as if responding to a second self, "now she's driving me to drink."

Rebecca opened her mouth to protest his imbibing. She stopped herself. Perhaps the liquor would cushion the shock of reality. "Lovers most certainly do fuss, fight, battle, make up and begin again. Your idea of love and being loved is an illusion. Grand passions are not like they are in storybooks."

"You're right as rain on that," he said morosely. "They put a good man through hell." And rendered a man not responsible for his actions. That's it! he thought. He wasn't so muddled after all. He stared at Rebecca, and as she stared back he was aware that she was seeing a spectrum of reality entirely beyond his field of vision. But there was a side to passion even she hadn't considered, he decided. The very definition of the word implied the impulse to freedom. He damned sure meant to keep his!

Rebecca correctly read the expression on his face and countered it. "You have a lot to learn, Parnell. Love is the pinnacle of human achievement. You're behaving as if it's some terrible affliction."

"I'm not interested in silly female claptrap. Let a man pay just one little bit of attention to a woman and first thing she does is dissect every little word and goings on."

"One little bit of attention? Is that what you're calling it? Well, I suppose you can't do otherwise and keep the image you have of yourself intact."

He turned away. Thwack! went the hatchet.

Rebecca left him to it. If ever there was such a thing as woman's rites, she was in the throes of it—with a man who was a particularly reluctant participant. He was discounting factors such as the irresistible chemistry they shared, that sex between them was good, that—well, there hadn't actually been that breathtaking meeting of minds. Warlike and crashing was more the description. Perhaps if she could see things more from his point of view.

Halfway to shore she turned about and retraced her steps. "Give me that flask," she demanded. He put his hand protectively over his back pocket.

"Nix that. This isn't the African Queen, you know."

"I want a drink."

"Oh yeah? And I'm the president's personal pilot."

"It's true. I do. I want to see what it does to my mind."

"In that case . . ." He unscrewed the top and handed her the flask. "I'm all for any improvement in the female mind."

The whiskey trailed fire as it slid down her throat and settled on the quarter slice of apple she'd consumed for breakfast. "Thank you."

"My pleasure. Notice any improvements?"

"Quite a few." She felt a burning behind her eyes. "One of which is a clarity of mind. I see things so-o-o clearly now. You're a disagreeable, obnoxious, insensitive snake-in-the-grass. You took advantage of me."

"I knew that was coming! By God, I knew it." He snatched the flask from her hand. "That was a waste of good whiskey."

Rebecca stared him down before she stalked out of the plane and headed toward the slew of gray boulders behind which she disposed of the apple and Jim Beam into the snow. So much for looking at issues from a man's point of view, she thought. Head aching, legs trembling, she hailed Nicholas and Molly. Together, the three of them staggered up the mountain to the cabin.

THE SEA RATIONS came with all sorts of wonderful things, the best of which were collapsible utensils from forks to frying pan.

Rebecca prepared a feast.

There was powdered milk, powdered coffee, powdered eggs and tubes of bacon paste to cook them with. There were sugar packets, salt packets, chunks of hard and bitter chocolate that she shaved and melted into hot milk. There were also packs of dried beef strips, malt tablets and several unlabeled boxes she meant to experiment with later. There were only four tin cups. She sipped boiled coffee laced with milk from the thermos cup.

Parnell drank his coffee from a tin can. He had laced it with the last dollop of Jim Beam, which was not enough to dull his senses. The earlier exchange with Rebecca had left him emotionally flattened. She was behaving as if everything was hunky-dory. Laughing, even. As if diddling with him had only been an amusing little whim.

Well, she wouldn't get another rise out of him! Of any kind. He was keeping to the edge of the activities, staying silent and looking inscrutable. It was only in the odd quiet moment that he was deluged with the memory of her straddling his groin and purring with pleasure.

Rebecca brought him a plate and sat next to him on the bunk to eat her own.

"There's no need to sit on top of me," he said.

Rebecca turned on him a lovely, wicked smile. "If I were on top of you," she said sotto voce so that it didn't carry to the children, "you wouldn't be interested in food."

"It's unseemly for a woman to brag about her sexual exploits," he said, then spent an uncomfortable moment dealing with the images her pithy remark evoked.

Though her cheeks were hot and flushed, as were unseen parts of her body, Rebecca's smile widened; her voice stayed low. "You mean it's okay to talk about sex while we're doing it, but afterward or before, you'd rather not?"

"Only certain types of women discuss—"

"What type is that?"

"You know."

"I don't. Perhaps after the kids are asleep you could enlighten me."

All of Parnell's prudence couldn't keep the words from his tongue. "Okay," he said, and delved into the food.

Every mouthful of food was savored, rolled on the tongue, swallowed with reverence.

Jonesy noisily scraped his plate. "I guess you could say this is our very first meal in our very own house."

"This isn't our house. We're only borrowing it," Rebecca said.

"We decided," said Nicholas. "We want to stay here."

"Yeah," put in Yancy. "Scrappy likes it here. He has lots of room to gallop."

"You could go get Abigail, couldn't you Rebecca?" Molly said. "You could bring her here. It's cheap. She wouldn't have to worry about money. We haven't had to spend any. Have we?"

One by one Rebecca took in the serious expressions on the young faces. "I'm proud of all of you," she said slowly. "You've faced up to adversity much better than I imagined you could. You've been a team and we've survived. But we have to go back. This isn't—"

Santee shifted on his haunches to face Rebecca. "Why do we have to go back? No one wants us. We could stay here. We could get books and teach ourselves. We could live off the land. I know we could. I'll bet there'll be rabbits in my traps in the morning. And that deer is still out there. I saw his tracks."

"And I'm getting around real good," announced Nicholas. "I know my way from the cabin down to the lake and back, by myself."

"I haven't wet the bed once since we've been here," reminded Molly. "Don't forget that."

Rebecca looked to Parnell for help. But he just sat cross-legged, pretending invisibility. He did lift the tin can perceptibly, as if in salute. Oh, great! Rebecca thought. Was she the only one among them with any practical sense left? Parnell expected romance to be all champagne and roses, man's finest hour. Now, the children, too, were playing at fairy tales.

"Listen to me, all of you. We're going back to Boise. If we aren't rescued by others, then we'll have to find our own way back. Captain Stillman is planning to hike out. We'll be going with him."

"No, you won't," he said, coming alive.

"You can't stop us. We'll follow you."

"I'm not going anywhere until after Santa comes," said Molly, defiantly. "If we keep moving around no telling where he'll leave my presents! Santee said if hasn't seen the SOS, his elves probably have."

Rebecca's face tightened. "We'll be back in Boise for Christmas. We're staying together. We got into this together. We'll get out together."

Santee was stoic. "We like it here."

"Perhaps one day we'll be able to come back," Rebecca offered.

"We won't," Jonesy said. "They don't let orphans have reunions. As soon as we're separated, that's it."

At the orphanage, Rebecca wore a number of hats, but in truth she wasn't a licensed social worker, only a housemother, an aide. Having been in the system most of their lives, the children knew more of the legal machinations than she. She sighed, defeated. "Under the circumstances, considering what you've all been through, that rule might not apply. Now come on, cheer up."

"How many days till Christmas?" asked Molly, her face recording her anxiety.

Rebecca looked to Parnell.

"Five," he said. He reached under the bunk and pulled out the rolls of maps and topographical charts.

Rebecca began to gather the dishes. "Think how sad Abigail must be, thinking we're all lost or dead," she said of the old dowager. "It's not fair to her that we stay here one minute, one day longer than necessary. Think how unhappy her Christmas would be."

Yancy stretched out on his stomach. "She was sending us off to find parents. She has to get rid of us. She doesn't have any money to keep us anyhow."

"That doesn't mean she doesn't love you."

"Nobody loves us," said Jonesy. "We're just commodities."

"I love you," Rebecca said.

"You get paid to."

"No, I don't. You can't put a price on love."

"Well, if you loved us," observed Molly, "you'd let us stay right here until after Santa comes." She stuck her thumb in her mouth and stared at the fire. Rebecca set aside the dishes and gathered the child into her lap.

"I do love you. If ever I have a little girl I'd want her to be just like you. Maybe not quite so sassy."

"Even with crippled feet?"

"One day your feet will be fixed."

"Would you let her suck her thumb?"

"I suppose."

"She'd have to watch out. It's not much good being somebody's little girl. God might take you."

Rebecca discovered her headache was returning. "There are worse places to be than with God." A platitude, she thought, ashamed of herself.

Molly sighed. "Yeah, and one of them's where Santa isn't."

THE LOPSIDED three-legged table now had four uneven legs. Parnell had hacked the three down and used one of them to create the fourth. The table was low, Chinese-style, and wobbly. But it created a surface for his unrolled maps. The boys hunkered around him. He found himself thinking aloud for Nicholas's benefit. The other boys easily followed the path his finger traveled over the charts.

"Where are we on the map?" Santee asked. Parnell pointed. "Somewhere in here, above forty degrees latitude and one hundred twenty degrees longitude." Which was twenty ground miles from the nearest highway in mountainous forest so thick the map only showed it as the Sierra Nevadas.

"How do you know for sure?"

"I don't," he answered and let his fingers trail down to Desolation Valley Wilderness. Not possible, he thought. Too far south.

"How are you gonna know which way to walk out?"

"If I head southwest, I'll come on a highway, eventually. North might take me deeper into the forest."

"North is where I'd like to head."

Parnell met Santee's dark eyes. "Don't even think it. I expect you to stay with Rebecca until I bring help. She won't be able to manage without you."

"I don't want to go back. Abigail can't keep us anymore. I've run away so much, I'll have to go to a juvenile home."

"Now's the time to stop running." Santee didn't appear convinced. Parnell heard himself say, "Look, when we get out of this mess, I'll look you up, maybe even teach you to fly. I've got this crop duster I've been meaning to put back together, you can help me."

"Then what?"

"I don't know." He was out of his depth and knew it. "Nobody can foretell the future."

"I can," snapped Rebecca as she carried a dozing Molly to her bunk. "The immediate future is everyone gets ready for bed. Adults excepted," she added icily. "The later future is we stay together, here or marching out."

Parnell jerked his thumb at the boys. "Hit it. I'll take care of this."

"I don't see how," said Jonesy. "Rebecca thinks she's the boss."

"Don't be a poop-head," said Yancy, willing to take his hero at his word. "If the captain said he'll take care of it, he will."

Beneath his beard, Parnell's cheeks felt parched. "I'll give her something else to think about."

Rebecca had no intention of debating Parnell while the boys kept their ears open or at her own expense. It was an hour before she was ready to give him the opportunity to "give her something else to think about."

The cabin reeked of wet wool and the tiny bar of Camay soap she'd put in a can of water to soften for morning ablutions. It went farther that way.

As she scraped the plates with snow by the door, stacked them on the counter and filled the water bin on the stove with snow to melt, she was aware that Parnell was watching her.

While his impatience grew she washed her face, brushed her teeth, tossed that water out and hung the shirt-cum-towel on a peg. From her cosmetic case she retrieved an emery board and when she finally sat cross-legged on the floor before the fire, she began filing her nails.

To Parnell the scrape of the nail file sounded like chalk screeching on a blackboard. It drove him nuts.

"Do you have to do that?"

"My nails are a wreck."

"It's putting my teeth on edge." He wanted to argue, but the expression on Rebecca's face was one of innocence—almost. Her hair and eyes seemed to suck up all the firelight, so that all else seemed dim. Her skin, he thought, was the rich color of cream, and he began to imagine kissing her on her neck. He raised his eyes and she was looking at him. He was afraid that she had a complete grasp of what was on his mind. Too quickly he lowered his head and tapped the chart, "I can't concentrate with that racket."

She put the nail file aside. "Get on with your bravado." She could see the comb marks in his hair where he'd wet it and slicked it down. He'd done a bit of preening when he thought she wasn't looking. "What is it you want me to think about?"

He stiffened. "That was just boy talk."

"How indifferent you men are."

"I don't know what you're accusing me of now, but if you want to fight, let's!"

"Wake the kids, why don't you?"

"I'm trekking out of here and you're not going!" he said in a hoarse whisper.

"In the interest of fairness I'll hear you out on the reasons why not."

"Alone, I can travel faster. And, have you noticed the snow. It's layered, the kind avalanches are made of. Who knows how high up the mountains I'll have to climb before . . . there aren't any sidewalks you know. A couple of the kids couldn't hack it."

"You can mark the path. We can keep up."

"It's impossible to talk any sense into you."

"I just have this feeling we should stay together. And we have to get back to Boise by Christmas. We just have to."

"What's Christmas? Just another day."

"You remind me of the boys. They pretend Christmas is nothing to them, but just watch their faces on Christmas morning when they're unwrapping presents. Up until the moment they have their gifts in their hands they're scared they won't get a Christmas. Many years they haven't."

"That's not me."

"Oh, I think it is. You want good things, you're just scared that when you get them they'll be snatched away."

"That's crazy."

"Tell me, how were you orphaned."

Parnell shrugged. "Same as a lot of kids. My dad was killed   in   the   Korean   conflict,   my   mother

kept . . . following the troops, so to speak. One day she
followed and left me behind."

Rebecca winced. "How old were you?"

"Thirteen."

She put her hand on his knee. "I'm sorry."

"Don't be. I made it."

"How?"

"Took to the road. It was easier to do back then.
There was always a commune of flower children willing to take in a stray. Uncle Henry caught up with me
a couple of years later." His voice softened. "He taught
me to fly. We did mostly crop dusting, a few air shows.
I wanted more and joined the Navy when I was sev-
enteen. I mustered out after twenty years. Had no place
to go except to Uncle Henry. He died and dumped the
airfield in my lap."

"Dumped? You love it."

"Belongs to creditors now."

Her hand was still on his knee.

"You can make a go of it, if you want to bad enough."

"Oh, I want all right." Much more than the airfield,
he thought, keeping an eye on her hand, watching for
any perceptible movement. He lifted his own leaden
hand and placed it atop hers, casual like.

Rebecca took the gesture much to heart. The glint in
her eyes was as if she knew of something exceedingly
satisfactory. Very softly, she said, "Shall we make up a
pallet in the other room?"

Parnell started, his heart leaped.

"Well, all right," he said. "I guess we could."

10

ONE OF THE MOST USEFUL ITEMS out of the locker was a thermal foil survival blanket. Parnell had pegged it over the doorway separating the rooms. One effect it had was keeping warmth in the bunkroom; the other was the privacy it afforded to anyone in the front room of the cabin. Rebecca wallowed in that privacy, not that she could speak above a whisper, but the blanket did afford the comfort of making the pallet in front of the stove. The woodbox door left open gave feeble light; it was enough by which to see Parnell's face.

"You look quite nice with a beard," she said, stroking it with her fingertips.

The compliment was heady stuff. Parnell was in bliss. "It's nothing but a flea catcher."

"I noticed there's some gray in it."

The bliss went.

"You're not one of those men who worries about aging are you? I think gray-streaked hair is distinguished looking."

He ran his hand down her naked back. She was so slender. He was enchanted by the svelte length of her, fitted next to him. A perfect alignment, he thought. He felt so relaxed, stretched out on the pallet. Her cheek rested on his chest. He stroked her shoulder and leaned down to kiss the top of her head, murmuring, "You make me crazy, Rebecca. You undo me. I can't even figure out who started this. Was it you?"

"I suppose it was a combination." She put her arms around him and kissed him. "So distinguished."

"A combustion, you mean." He massaged the delicate vertebrae that protruded down her back. "If you kiss me like that you're only going to get me started again." There was a slight but obvious movement of her hips against his thigh.

"Oh? Well how about if I kiss you like this?" She buried her face in his chest, her tongue flicked out, touching his nipple."

"Hey!"

"Shhhh. You do it to me."

"That's . . . different . . ."

She drew the tip of his nipple into her mouth and sucked.

"Dear me," Parnell groaned. He loved how affectionate she was. The idea of having that, day in and day out, was beginning to have solid appeal to him. He imagined what she'd be like in a real bed, with true privacy. He didn't think he'd be able to stand it. It was the wrong kind of imagery. Wishful thinking. For all her "making do" since the crash, in his mind she was a champagne-and-silk kind of woman. He was Jim Beam and oily rags.

Her mouth left his nipple. He felt her tongue on his ribs. The hand that had been at his neck moved in a slow downward spiral until it reached the juncture of his thighs where he began to swell almost immediately. The philosophy of silk and rags left his mind. He made a noise in his throat.

Soft laughter erupted from Rebecca. "I thought that'd bring you back."

"I wasn't anywhere."

"You weren't here. Does my lovemaking bore you?"

"Bore me? You're the most exciting thing that's ever happened to me."

"What were you thinking about then?"

"I was asking myself how much of you I could bear."

Rebecca raised her head. "What was your answer?"

He pressed his arms about her. "As much of you as you'll give me."

"Suppose it's all of me?"

His stomach tightened in alarm. It was a question on two levels. He'd cut his tongue out before he admitted love. As soon as they got back to civilization she'd go off to silk and he back to oily rags. Then where would he be? Off in broken-heart land, that's where. As it was, he'd be months getting his libido under control again.

"Suppose?" he tossed back playfully. But to dissuade her of further talk he brought her face to him and kissed her, his tongue thrusting between her lips. Rebecca's breath caught in her throat. He was engorged and pressing between her legs. He pulled her body higher and penetrated her. For a long moment he held her there, unmoving.

"Something wrong?" she asked, voice thick.

"Enjoying," he whispered into her ear.

"We'll always remember this won't we?"

"I couldn't live long enough to forget."

"I love you," she said softly.

"I—I was talking about knee and elbow burns."

He sounded forlorn and vulnerable. Rebecca laughed, the sound of her laughter melded with the crackling fire, the winter wind bracketing the cabin, Parnell's involuntary intake of breath.

"Were you? Poor darling. You're body's really had the worst of it. Shall we stop?" She tightened her muscles; felt the length of him respond inside her.

"Don't tease me like that."

She rubbed against him, then leaned forward and kissed him lightly on the ear, taking his earlobe between her teeth and gently sucking on it. "You're so strong . . ."

"Stop that. Keep still," he said, his voice huskier than before.

"But I want you so . . . Here, suppose I just do this?"

"Oh, Lord—" His back arched.

"We're meant for each other. You know that don't you?"

"I don't know anything. I can't think."

"Perhaps I ought to just let you get some sleep."

"Move off this pallet and I'll break your ankle," he muttered through clenched teeth.

She rose up on an elbow. "I'm not a violent person."

"Could you please just shut up?"

"But I thought you wanted to talk."

"This is what I want," he said, demonstrating.

REBECCA CAME AWAKE slowly. The smell of boiling coffee was in the air. For a brief drowsy moment she thought herself at the orphanage, imagined she could hear the chatter of the children down the hall in the great old farmhouse kitchen where so much of their living took place. Imagined she could hear Abigail chastising one child or another on table manners. The alien hardness of the bunk intruded, striking the chord of reality. The fragrance of the coffee remained, but the cabin was quiet. Too quiet. She raised her head and discovered herself alone.

She dressed, thrusting her arms into her coat as she went outside. It was easy to pick out Molly's footsteps in the snow. They lead up to the outhouse. "Molly?"

"Went all by myself," the child answered.

"Where is everybody?"

"I don't know. But nobody would let me go with them."

"What did the captain say to you?"

"He said, stay with you till you woke up."

"Then what?"

"Then I had to go to the bathroom."

"How long has he been gone?"

"You know I can't tell time. Are you gonna fix breakfast now?"

"In a minute. I'll walk you back to the cabin. If the boys show up, tell them I said stay put until I get back."

"I don't want to stay by myself. A bear might get me."

"All the bears are asleep."

"That's not what Santee said. He said only mother bears sleep all winter. Daddy bears don't."

"Santee isn't the last word on bears! Now please, I've got to find the captain." Suppose he's left us! Rebecca thought, recalling how he'd brushed aside her anxieties at being left alone in the wilderness with the children. She glanced at the sky.

The sun was shining, gray-tinted clouds hugged the mountain peaks. Nearby a pair of birds chattered. She settled Molly with a hard cracker in front of the fireplace.

"A bear is gonna get me and I'll be dead and you'll be sorry," she complained.

Rebecca dipped into the pan of coffee on the stove and took a sip to fortify herself against the cold, against the anxiety that was creeping up her spine. "I'm just going down to the lake."

It was a futile excursion. No one was there. The door to the plane had been closed. She couldn't get it open. Behind her the SOS glared bright orange in the snow. It did no good. There was only herself to see it.

When she returned to the cabin, the boys were clustered under the lintel. Santee was not among them.

"Rebecca, look!" Jonesy said. At his feet was the skinned carcass of a rabbit. "Santee must've trapped it."

"Where is he? Where's the captain?" She watched the boys exchange glances. Her heart slid into her stomach. "They've gone off together, haven't they? Left us here?"

"Santee said he wasn't going back, you'd have to find him first."

"And Captain Stillman? What did he say?" He had betrayed her. Used her! Made love to her and escaped while she was wallowing in the afterglow.

"That we'd all better mind you or he'd skin us alive," said Jonesy. He poked the rabbit with his shoe. "You think that's what we'd look like skinned?"

"He said he'd take Scrappy to the glue factory," said Yancy.

"And that he didn't have anything against whipping a blind kid," put in Nicholas.

Rebecca visualized Parnell lining up the kids, passing out orders, making threats, dishing it all up with a dash of bravado, then going off and leaving her with the consequences. He was probably laughing his head off.

"Do you know how to cook a rabbit?" asked Jonesy.

Rebecca looked down at the skinned pink carcass. She felt squeamish. "No."

"It's protein. We need protein, you said."

"I wonder what Santee did with the skin?" Nicholas said.

"He's probably gonna make himself a coat out of it," suggested Yancy.

"It takes more than one fur, stupid."

"Stop it!" Rebecca said, ushering them all inside. The rabbit carcass caused Molly to squeal and retire under a mound of clothes to her bunk, thumb in mouth.

"Fat lot of pioneers all of you would make!" Rebecca said. She scooped up the rabbit, held it at arm's length. "We'll boil it."

"Roasted would be better. In cowboy movies they always roast it over a fire."

"Well, we're not in a cowboy movie. We're just lost." A sob broke from her throat. "We're lost and we're going to stay lost. We're going to die."

Alarmed, the boys backed away from her. Molly covered her head.

"Oh, don't pay any attention to me, I'm just scared. I don't know how I can find Santee. I'm mad at the captain for going off without us."

"He'll be back. He likes us," volunteered Nicholas.

"I'll hold that thought."

A half dozen times she scoured the area around the cabin and the lake trying to spot Santee. She visited the old campsite in hopes of finding him there. But the snow near it was virgin and untrampled. She told herself he'd show up by dark. Behind the cabin she found tracks leading upward to a southern ridge. The size of them suggested they were Parnell's.

At dusk the leafless trees were engraved in clarity; blue-black shadows. A northerly breeze whipped up the snow. Rebecca felt an ache in her throat. She missed Parnell. She'd taken so much strength from his presence that now she felt detached in some odd way. As if she'd been severed from all that was important to her.

The seemingly deserted winterscape was alive with night sounds she couldn't identify. She stared unblinking at the footsteps until shadows overtook them. She had a strange whisper of dread. She wouldn't allow her brain to tell her the feeling was for Parnell. He was fine. He knew how to take care of himself. His Navy training was bred into him. The dread was for herself, for the children.

She wrapped her arms around herself and waited for her life to pass before her eyes. Her only vision was those hours spent in Parnell's arms, the lovely way he made her feel so much a woman.

Just get us all out of this alive, she broadcast to Heaven, *and I won't ever complain again—at least not to You. When I catch up to Parnell Stillman I'll take care of him all by myself!*

Inside the cabin she hung her coat on a peg. "I think we're going to be all right," she said.

"What about Santee?" came the chorus.

"Him, too. He's smart. He can handle himself. I'm sure he'll show up soon. He knows I'd worry."

"What about Captain Stillman?"

Rebecca poked angrily at the rabbit with the bent-tine fork. "Nothing about him! He's the stupidest, most uncaring man I've ever met. I'm going to tell him so the first chance I get."

The first chance she got came as she was dipping up the first serving of rabbit. Parnell burst through the door roaring in fury and dragging an unhappy-looking Santee by the coat collar. The cabin echoed with his anger.

"This is the thanks I get! I promised to help this kid, teach him to fly. He gave me his word that he wouldn't slip off. Found him across the lake on that north ridge."

"I was tracking that old deer!"

"Bull-doody! You were setting up a camp."

"Tell him, Rebecca. I found droppings. I was building a blind! I told Molly to tell—"

"Don't blame me! I'm too little to remember everything. I'm only five."

Rebecca couldn't speak or deny or verify. The tube of her throat had closed up. Relief was jackknifing through her, the sensation coming from far away, as if borrowed and unfamiliar.

She dropped the cup; it disappeared into the pot of thin rabbit stew. "Oh! Look what you made me do," she wailed.

Parnell took in her stricken expression: the eyes huge, the slender neck so taut the hollows at her throat deepened. He could see her pulse beating. He put his arm around her and led her to a bunk. "Hey! Calm down. We're all safe."

"I don't feel like calming down! I thought you'd left us."

He shook his head. "I scouted the ridges above the treeline. We'd feel pretty stupid if we walked out of here in one direction only to discover there was a highway or road beyond a ridge we hadn't checked.

"Was there?"

"Nope."

"You said we . . . That means we're not fighting anymore about who's going, who's staying?"

"You've convinced me. Staying together is the best policy." Staying together. It had been in his mind the entire long and tiring day. Rebecca was for evermore a part of the fabric of his life now. There was no undoing it. He looked down at her, smiling, conscious of his height beside her smallness. He wanted to tell her, watch her reaction, but pride held him back—and an awareness of the children standing in a semicircle, staring and listening to every damned word! Declaring himself in front of an audience was asking too much! Anyway, he didn't have the words right. And even if he had, Rebecca didn't look to be in a mood to hear them. "Well!" he said brightly. "I'm starved. What's for supper?"

SHE HAD A CHOICE, Rebecca told herself. She could start a fight and ruin what promised to be a nice evening. Or, she could just forget about being angry.

The rabbit stew had been a bit thin, but she'd picked the meat off the bones and seasoned it with the bacon paste. It had made even the hard crackers taste satisfactory. Not a drop was left and Parnell had been effusive with his compliments for both Rebecca and Santee.

Santee strutted with importance at providing the meal. He had managed to convince Parnell that he really had lost track of time, building the deer blind.

The boy had gone off to his bunk weary, but happy. The other children had followed suit.

Parnell was studying his charts, plotting their passage out, but Rebecca knew he was keeping a wary eye on her.

And so he should! She was most annoyed with him for being gone all day, then treating her so cavalierly. She'd worried herself sick! But she could feel herself giving in. Her acquiescence made her angry at herself.

"You might as well spit it out," Parnell said, not looking up.

"Do you really want to know?"

"I asked, didn't I?"

"I'm angry, that's what."

"No foolin'."

"You're being condescending."

He decided to wait that one out.

"I'm annoyed at your attitude toward me, at the way you just went off today without telling me. That was inconsiderate."

"You were asleep."

"You could've awakened me."

"I started to. But you looked so . . ."

"So, what?"

"Fragile, I guess. And don't expect me to keep on saying stuff like that."

Fragile? She'd never been thought fragile or delicate before. It implied that she needed someone to take care of her. She'd always taken care of herself. "I was worried. I went looking for you."

"I'm not used to anybody worrying about me."

He stared at the fire a long time, the silence creating a strange nearness between them rather than a gulf.

Rebecca watched him. She was suddenly afraid of what
he was going to say next.

Finally, he looked at her; he smiled a little half-smile.
"I might know a cure for worry."

"Oh?"

"I'll make us some hot chocolate."

Rebecca gazed at him in disbelief.

"We could drink it in there." He tilted his head toward the other room.

"You just want sex," she whispered.

"I just want to do something nice for you."

She let out a deep breath. "As it happens," she said
slowly, "I'd like for you to do something nice for me,
too.... But, Parnell?"

"What?"

"Forget the hot chocolate."

IT TOOK TWO DAYS to prepare to leave. All that they
couldn't carry out had to be hauled down to the plane
and stored. The children's totes were converted into
backpacks in which to carry the sea rations. Walking
sticks were cut and trimmed for each. The great yellow
raft was laid out in the snow and painstakingly cut into
rectangles for makeshift ponchos. Parnell instructed
everyone to wear two sets of clothes. He gave up his
socks once again to Rebecca and fashioned for himself
foot wrappings out of a shirt.

The sun was only a pink glow in the eastern sky when
the fires in the stove and hearth were put out for the last
time. Parnell drained the dregs of his coffee and looked
at Rebecca. He was in a lousy mood. "That's it, then,"
he said.

She took one last glance about the cabin. "In a way I hate to leave after we've finally caught the rhythm of living in the wilderness.

Santee hung the traps he'd brought in on the pegs. They'd been empty that morning. "I'm going to come back one day."

Rebecca lay her hand on his arm. "I feel the same way. Perhaps some summer..."

"If we're going, let's go!" announced Molly. "I gotta be somewhere Santa knows where I am before Christmas Eve."

"Fall in!" Parnell yelled.

Rebecca jerked. "Do you have to scream like that? We're none of us deaf, you know." His face was flushed, his dark hair curled over his forehead. "You feel all right?"

"I feel fine. Let's move out." He was anxious about the strenuous activity that faced them. He had the notion Rebecca was going to see him in a different light once they were back in their own lives, on their own turf. He suspected she wouldn't give him a second glance. All that night as he slept, he had dreamt of her... kissing her, lying at her side. He had awakened with a dull ache that refused to go away.

He could feel her eyes on him as he checked his pockets for folded maps, the compass, the tin of matches. The hatchet as well as the gun were tucked into his belt. "What're you staring at?"

"Nothing!"

"That's what I thought."

"Why are you trying to start a fight now?"

"We don't have time to indulge your whims. Let's get the show on the road."

"Whims?" she thrust at him, but he refused to be provoked.

Outside the cabin with the door closed firmly behind them, Parnell looked over his motley entourage. Santee's face was pinched. "You and I will take turns at leading and bringing up the rear. You take point first," he told the boy. "But set us a fast pace. I want to be out of this valley and atop the first ridge by nightfall." He turned to Rebecca. "You all set?"

"I look like a Laplander. I feel stupid," she said of the way she wore the only skirt she'd packed over her slacks.

"Leave it to a woman to worry about what she looks like in the middle of nowhere," he scoffed. "You'll be glad of the warmth later." He reached out to touch her. He would have to live with things whatever the outcome. No sense buying misery, he thought, dropping his hand.

Rebecca sensed the distance he was putting between them. He was having second thoughts about her! As she felt her heart sinking she turned away to touch the cabin door. It was forever shut on a part of their lives.

But inside the spare ramshackle cabin she'd found something she'd been looking for for a long long time. She wasn't about to let go of it so easily.

Molly skipped ahead, so she took Nicholas's hand.

"I'm set," she said and dug her walking stick into the snow.

STRUNG OUT YARDS APART they climbed, crawled and hobbled up the twisting course behind Santee. It seemed to Rebecca they had to stop every few minutes on the hopeless wild inhospitable mountainside to catch their breath in the thinning air. When Parnell finally called a halt, she collapsed in the snow. "My legs," she moaned. She stretched them out in front of her and watched them tremble.

His face inscrutable, Parnell knelt beside her and massaged first one leg, then the other. "How's that?"

It was the most impersonal ministration Rebecca had ever been subjected to. "Heaven," she cooed lightly. "Now if only there was a sauna!"

Parnell forgot himself. "You like all that fancy stuff?"

"It's nice if it's available. I can live without it. Why?"

He sat back on his haunches. "Just making conversation."

"Save your breath." When his brows knit together in a frown she started to smile to take the sting out of her words, but changed her mind. If he was going to revert to type, so could she.

"I think I'm gonna get rid of Scrappy," Yancy said with a long sigh. "He's a horse and I can't even ride him. I wish I had a real horse! Then I could go up and down the mountains faster 'n' faster."

"Scrappy's been a good friend to you," Rebecca said with caution.

"I know. But he's a lot of work. And anyway, can't anybody else see him but me. Abigail keeps saying I ought to put him out to pasture. If I get worried about anything I can always go and talk to him."

"When we get back you can talk to Abigail about it."

"I'd like to see the look on her face when she finds out we're alive," said Jonesy.

"I bet the whole world thinks we're dead!" came from Nicholas and was voiced with glee.

Molly started. "If Santa thinks I'm dead, he'll give my presents away!"

"Santa's like God," Parnell said. "He knows if you're dead or alive."

Rebecca's eyes widened. "Parnell! What a sweet thing to say."

His cheeks and brow flamed. "I was just trying to avoid histrionics. Get up everybody. March!"

Within two hours Molly's legs had given out. Parnell carried her on his shoulders. By dusk, their faces and hands were chapped by the cold dry air, their ears so frozen just to touch one brought tears. It took ten hours to crest the ridge Parnell had scouted in four.

They found shelter under a shelf of rock on the southern face of the mountain. It was not quite a cave; it was perhaps five feet from floor to ceiling at its entrance and eight feet deep into the mountain. The floor was free of snow, but littered with sticks and leaves. It held a vague scent of animal musk.

"Home for the night," groaned Parnell as he lowered Molly to the ground.

Amid ooohs and aaaahs of relief the boys flopped helter-skelter about the cave. "I knew it," moaned Jonesy as he peeled off his shoes and socks. "Blisters! And they're all raw."

As she let her makeshift backpack, which was Parnell's flightbag, slide from her shoulders, Rebecca peered into the gloomy depths of the shelter. "If I sit down I'll never get up."

"I can get a fire going," Santee volunteered, raking a pile of dry leaves with his hands.

"My nose is frozen," announced Nicholas. His cheeks were scarlet and wind-whipped. Rebecca put her hands to her own numbed cheeks. She longed for the warmth and primitive comfort of the cabin they'd left behind.

Parnell looked first at Nicholas then inspected Jonesy's feet. "We're going to have to find some way to protect ourselves better from frostbite."

"Is my nose gonna fall off?"

"I don't think so, sport." He motioned to Rebecca. "You think you can have a look at everyone's feet?" He tossed the first-aid kit to her. "Blisters are going to be as much an enemy as the cold."

It was an agony for Rebecca to bend her legs to squat. Her stomach griped from hunger. She squinted against the pain and drew cold air through her clenched teeth.

"I shouldn't have insisted we all go out together. I was wrong. I don't think the children have the stamina. I don't think I do. It's suicide."

"Belay that!" Parnell growled. "It was my decision. Mine alone. If I didn't think we could all march out of here, I would've insisted you stay behind." He watched her begin applying the antiseptic. "Use that topical anesthetic on everyone's feet, too."

Rebecca turned her face up to him. "But look at us!"

"I'll figure something out, a better way for us to travel."

"Like hitch Scrappy to a sleigh?"

"Not too much is wrong with you. Your tongue's still sharp."

Rebecca sniffed. "The tongue is always the last to go."

Parnell unzipped the flight bag, drew out the pans, the packets of powdered eggs, milk, chocolate. He moved slowly, his shoulders ached, a stiffness was settling in from the unfamiliar burden of Molly. "You rest for an hour. I'll see to the food."

Rebecca lifted an eyebrow, but called the younger boys and Molly to lie down next to her. It was a measure of how weary they all were that no one complained of the way hard rough rock bit into elbow and hip bone. She unfolded the thermal foil blanket and spread it over them all. At the mouth of the overhang, the leaves and twigs flickered into flames. In the darkness beyond an owl hooted.

The firelight cast Parnell's shadow on the ceiling. For a moment Rebecca watched it. He was being only as nice as circumstances dictated—less, perhaps—reverting to the insensitive clod he'd been when she'd first laid eyes on him. She hoped he didn't carry it too far. She'd get mad. But at the moment she didn't have the strength to squeak, much less squawk. She closed her eyes and succumbed to exhaustion.

When she next stirred it was because Parnell was shaking her awake, roughly so.

"Let me sleep," she protested.

"Like hell! I did that once. You chewed me out." He grabbed her hands, pulled her to her feet and shoved her toward the fire. A plate of eggs, very browned, and a tin of coffee were on the rock floor. "Go eat."

The kids were sprawled every which way, curled up on the strips of yellow raft and covered with their coats. Rebecca picked her way over them. They've toughened, she thought, or perhaps they were more adaptable. Bones and muscles she didn't know existed within her ached from lying upon bedrock. She stepped beyond the fire, scooped up snow and rubbed it on her face.

While she ate, Parnell sat gazing into the fire, knees up, elbows resting on them with his hands hanging down between them. He didn't look happy.

"You're worried aren't you?" she challenged.

He didn't look at her. He felt like telling her, just to see what she'd say. He had one foot in paradise, one in hell and he didn't know which way to jump. But it seemed to him with every step away from the cabin she'd begun lapsing again into the kind of woman that made his stomach hurt. If only he could be more direct—but it just wasn't in him. He sighed glumly. Even knowing that, he couldn't help himself from being attracted to her. He could feel it between his legs.

"I was just thinking about the plane," he said when he discovered she was still waiting for an answer.

"Isn't it insured? I thought—"

"I'll replace her, but buying used planes isn't like going to your corner used-car lot. Boeing doesn't build her class anymore. She was a good airship. Amos and I reconditioned her ourselves."

There was something in his tone. Rebecca tried to lock onto it and couldn't. "I'm a little scared—about going back," she admitted.

"Why?"

"Won't there be publicity?"

"I imagine we're old news by now."

"Be practical. Five orphans, a single woman, a single man, we show up after almost two weeks in the wilderness . . ." Her voice trailed off.

He drew in a sharp breath. "If you're asked, just stick to the basics. Don't mention—"

"Don't mention what?" But she knew what he meant. Forget their relationship. Forget that they'd fallen in love. Forget the lovemaking. Don't mention... "Of course," she said.

"Well, it wouldn't look good, would it?" he said, filled with misery, aching to tell her he didn't give a hoot in hell if she shouted it for the world to hear.

Her mouth was suddenly dry. "No, it wouldn't," she said stiffly.

Their eyes locked.

Rebecca waited for him to say that it didn't matter what people thought, that they were going to get married.

Parnell waited for Rebecca to say that she loved him no matter what, that she didn't care whatever anyone thought.

He shrugged to accommodate the sore muscles in his shoulders. Rebecca read the gesture wrong. She looked away.

"Well, I guess that's it then," Parnell said.

Rebecca looked down at the empty plate in her hand. She'd eaten without tasting a thing. "I guess I'd better see to my own feet before I sack out," she said.

"I'll help you."

"That won't be necessary."

"I don't mind."

"I don't want you to touch me!"

Parnell winced. "Of course. I understand. *See? he told himself. Love hurts!*

11

PARNELL'S BETTER WAY to travel was for him to forge ahead. Where the rest of them were to stop at noon or as close as he could judge it, he would arrange firewood, ready for the match. Then he would move on until just before dusk to locate a suitable campsite for the night.

Rebecca suspected his reason in that method. He wanted to distance himself from her.

They weren't even looking at each other when they spoke now. Words were cast into the air at shoulder level or staring at the ground or while she helped this child or that adjust a backpack or tie a shoelace.

"Aren't you going to take some food?" she asked. It was an innocuous question and meant to engage him in conversation and put his leaving off.

"I filled the thermos with coffee. It'll do me until you catch up." There was a nervousness in his voice that she had not heard before. He seemed almost insecure. "You won't have any trouble following my trail in the snow."

"I don't like it. Suppose one of us gets hurt? Suppose you do?"

"Send Santee to get me."

"Well, suppose it's Santee who's hurt?"

"Listen damn it! Quit buying trouble. That's all you women do. You're making my stomach hurt."

Rebecca didn't like the slant of his innuendo. He was back to lumping her with other women he'd known; the ones who had made him unhappy. She summoned every ounce of self-control, forcing an attitude of amiable nonchalance.

"Well, by the time we catch up to you, I expect you to have the campsite ready, beds folded down, supper in the pot. We'll be worn out you know, tramping the forest."

"Very funny."

She couldn't just let him go like this. She had no idea what she felt for him anymore. A sense of terror overtook her. "Why are you doing this to me, to us?"

"You want to get back to Boise, don't you?"

"That's not what I meant."

Distractedly, Parnell turned away. She was tearing him up. Yet all he could think of was that once returned to their ordinary lives, she wouldn't give him a second glance. He remembered how she'd looked at him when he'd first encountered her. Like something she would scrape off a shoe.

"What did you mean?" he finally said.

Rebecca was afraid to put it into words. If she did he might distance himself even further. She felt as if a weight were crushing her chest. "You never tell me how you feel about anything."

"I feel like finding a way out of here. That suit you?"

"Why are you being so stubborn, so obtuse?"

"I want out of here." He was infatuated, he thought. That was his problem. Never before had he wanted to give so much of himself to a woman. Not only sensuality, but tenderness. It just didn't fit the image he had of himself. He was lean and mean and tough. He was

forgetting himself because Rebecca was bent on capti-
vating him. The way he was thinking, the airy sensation in his gut was all her fault.

Rebecca stiffened. To say more would be resorting
to begging. She couldn't do that. Pleading had been too
much a part of her earlier life. She hadn't liked herself
then. She'd spent years building her self-esteem, learning to like herself, learning to become independent, and
since the crash—strong. She picked up her walking
stick, called to the orphans.

"Let's get out of here, then," she said to Parnell. "Do
whatever it takes. Which direction are we going in today?"

For the first hour they trekked together. In some
places the snow lay thigh-high. And though Parnell
forged a path of sorts, it was hard work to force her
body through it. Often, she leaned into a drift and fell
rather than walked forward. But as Molly began to tire
and Jonesy's blisters began to trouble him Parnell pulled
ahead. When he disappeared around a heap of scree
Rebecca called out to him. He turned back, lifted a
hand, then disappeared again.

Rebecca sagged. That was it. He'd left them behind.
"We'll stop and rest here for a minute," she told the
others.

"I think I'd be better off walking barefoot," Jonesy
said.

"Who's going to carry me?" Molly wanted to know.

"I'm scared," said Nicholas. "I don't understand why
nobody found us."

Santee helped the unseeing boy to a downed tree.
"Because they didn't look."

"Of course they looked," Rebecca chastised as she lowered herself to the log. "I'm sure when we get to a telephone, we'll discover that hundreds of people searched for us."

Yancy plunked down next to Nicholas. "They sure didn't look in the right place."

Rebecca smiled. "No they didn't. But we found ourselves, didn't we? We never really felt lost, did we? Anyway, it was an adventure. Just think of the stories you can tell when you go back to school."

Jonesy cried as he unstuck first one and then the other sock from his heels. "I'll never make it. How far do we have to hike anyway?"

"I don't know. But you will make it. We'll all make it." Rebecca liberally applied the topical anesthetic to the broken blisters. "Put your shoes back on."

A dark cloud crossed the sun, the mountainside went suddenly dark. She scowled at the wintry sky. "Come on. Let's hurry."

As they moved up, following in Parnell's footsteps, the terrain became more formidable. Trees stood high out of the snow, bent and gnarled by the constant wind. Once they came upon where Parnell had backtracked, he'd drawn an arrow in the snow, pointing to the correct path. The link reassured Rebecca. Eventually they came upon a second snow-formed arrow. It pointed to a protective outcropping of rock. Behind it they found a small pile of brush. Rebecca fumbled with the precious matches, lighting the fire. They all sank about it wearily.

"Who's hungry?" she asked brightly.

Nobody was.

"Let's go back to the cabin," Yancy pleaded. "I'm cold."

Rebecca took out the thermal foil blanket. They all hunched beneath it. She put her arms around the blind and the lame. "We can't go back. We're going forward. There may be a road over that next ridge. The captain may be waiting for us this very minute."

When they caught up with him, she wouldn't let him go on ahead anymore. She didn't care about being independent. She couldn't do this, couldn't keep encouraging the kids, cajoling them, pushing them to take another step, then another. She didn't care about her pride anymore.

The fire died. There wasn't another piece of wood to add. Parnell had probably judged the time it would take to burn down. She used her walking stick to drag herself to her feet.

Each forward step was a chore. Molly whimpered. The pain of it all emotionally, physically was nearly too much. Rebecca was so short of breath she kept having to take big gulps of the frigid air. When her voice gave out, Santee had to take over. She couldn't help being proud of him. He talked them up and around the mountain—always in Parnell's footsteps.

When it became so dark they could hardly see, she called a halt. Santee pointed. "Look! Look there!" he shouted, directing her gaze down the mountainside. "There's a glow. I'll bet it's a fire. The captain has set up camp there."

And then out of the darkness Parnell materialized. "I could hear you a mile off," he said.

"If it's another mile, none of us will make it," Rebecca choked.

"I found a road." He wore his face like a mask, but Rebecca heard an undertone of controlled excitement in his voice.

"Well . . . hooray," she said.

He stood mute for a moment, then hefted Molly, picked up his flight bag and strode off toward the camp he'd made.

"Hey, Captain," Jonesy called after him. "You gonna come back and carry me?"

"Afraid you'll have to manage for yourself, sport."

Jonesy sniffed. "Nobody likes a fat kid."

All their old fears and hang-ups were coming back, Rebecca thought. "Go ahead and take off your shoes, Jonesy," she said. "I don't expect you'll come down with pneumonia in the distance between here and camp."

"Okay," he said. "But I bet I'm the only orphan in the world with blubber who's tough enough to hike through snow and woods."

"That's enough. All of you. You've survived an event other kids would give their eyeteeth to have experienced."

"You think so?"

"Of course. You're all heros."

"Hey!" said Nicholas. "Maybe they'll make a movie about us!"

Rebecca rolled her eyes. "I hardly expect we've caused that much attention." She hoped and prayed not. Some publicity was inevitable, but the idea of television crews and newspaper reporters made her shudder. Her face felt hot just under the skin, but icy on the surface. She'd have to bring up the subject of themselves with Parnell. Make sure they had their stories straight. She couldn't bear it if suddenly the whole world knew she'd been rejected by a man a second time in her life.

By the time they reached the campsite, Parnell was stirring an egg-snow mixture into a froth with a peeled stick. He'd constructed a simple lean-to on a small bit of level ground below a large overhang of rock. It sheltered their backs from the cold breeze. In minutes, with their faces leaning toward the cheery fire, they were warm and lethargic.

Rebecca forced herself to scoop up snow to melt for hot chocolate. "Seems like old times," she said.

"Meaning?" Parnell asked cautiously.

"This is how we started out, melting snow. I guess you could say we've come full circle." She felt his eyes on her, but she didn't look up to read what might be in them. Parnell's socks were much too big for her, and one had slipped down inside her boot and rode painfully against her ankle. She sat back down to remedy the problem. Suddenly the cold and her own bleak exhaustion overwhelmed her. She rested her forehead on her knee and squeezed her eyes shut tightly. Damn it! She loved him. He was being such an ass. Insufferable!

Parnell was trying to serve up the eggs and watch what Rebecca was doing at the same time. When she put her head down on her knees, prickles crawled up his neck. He squirmed inside. He knew what she was up to all right! She was trying to make him feel guilty. Every woman he'd ever known had a knack for doing that. They did it just to make him miserable. Get him to suck up to her. It wasn't him that had called it off. Rebecca had done it with all her screeching. Don't touch me, don't touch me! Hadn't he told her that he couldn't get enough of her? What'd she want him to do anyway? Beg? Get down on his knees? To hell in a basket with that! He was better off pretending nothing had happened.

Under self-inflicted duress, he shoved a plate of eggs at her. "You want to eat or what?

Rebecca lifted her head. "Don't take that tone with me. It's not my fault we've been stuck out here."

Hostility got the better of him, he slammed the plate at her feet. Eggs flew. "Seems like I've heard that song before."

"So have we," muttered Santee.

"Keep outta this," Parnell snarled.

"Why are y'all fussing again?" asked Nicholas.

Delicately, with her fingertips, Rebecca picked bits of egg out of the snow, arranging them on the plate. "We're just having a discussion. It has nothing to do with any of you. But in the interest of harmony, the captain and I will chat later."

"Suits me," Parnell agreed, his face filled with mistrust and apprehension. Overcome with a sensation of helplessness, which he didn't like, he built up the fire and sat opposite Rebecca. The flames towered so that he couldn't see across to her. Out of sight, out of mind, he told himself.

By the time the fire had died down, the kids had curled up to sleep in the lean-to. When Parnell raised his eyes he found himself faced with Rebecca's accusing stare. "Don't try to make me the scapegoat," he warned.

Rebecca glared at him, a good imitation of his own ferocious bulldog expression. "You mean about the crash?"

"I take full responsibility on that score. I'm talking about the other."

She felt bands tighten in her chest. The ache almost took her breath away. "I won't mention it, if you don't."

"The kids didn't notice anything." It was a statement, spoken to reassure himself that his tough exterior image would remain intact.

"Probably not."

"We were discreet." He watched her pupils contract into tiny black specks.

"Oh, shut up," she said, barely audible because she was on the verge of tears.

A cold sweat suddenly drenched Parnell's brow. He had a galloping urge to gather her into his arms, croon sweet things into her ear, put his hand under her sweater. He restrained himself, but he had to move. He stirred around, made up a brush bed for her next to Molly under the lean-to. "You ought to get some sleep," he said.

"You, too," she managed, and after a moment went to lie down.

"I think I'll keep the fire going for a while." It would cut down on dream time, he thought. No sense letting a fantasy get the best of him. Overhead a break in the clouds revealed a star-studded sky, a hanging slice of moon. The fantasy came anyway.

He could see himself waking up mornings, Rebecca's head on his pillow, her body arched, fitted into the curve of his. But he'd probably have to marry her to make that fantasy real. The first time he'd been married he hadn't had to raise the question. One night he'd gone over to Frieda's and she had told him she'd made arrangements with the chaplain. Most of his clothes and shaving kit were already at her place. At the time it seemed the right thing to do.

Somehow, he couldn't see Rebecca making such an assumption. She'd want it to be a joint decision. Hah! He could just see himself asking.

"Dear, how would you like to get hitched?" He shook his head. That sounded like he was trying to harness a horse to a wagon.

Maybe: *"Say Rebecca, since we've already been... you know—wanna get married?"* Not romantic enough, and above all women wanted romance.

"Darling... ?" He couldn't even start the question out that way! He'd never called a woman darling in his life. She'd probably laugh him right out of the room.

Then what?

He stared down at his hands. They were trembling. Coward! Jell-O gut, he named himself.

Rebecca slept. He watched her, transfixed, until he'd convinced himself that the real fantasy had been the hours he'd spent with her on the pallet in the cabin.

THE SUN CAME UP all brazen and cheerful as if there wasn't a bit of misery or hunger anywhere in the world. Rebecca stared at the sky as if betrayed. When she turned that same stare on Parnell, he avoided looking at her. She just couldn't let him get off that easily. The good sleep she'd had renewed her courage. What had been done could not be undone. Could not be forgotten. She opened her mouth to tell him, and finally she burst out, "It won't work, you know, pretending nothing's changed, pretending there's nothing between us."

His face went rigid with panic. "I don't know what you're talking about."

"Yes, you do. And that's the point I'm trying to make." She took off the overskirt and shoved it into a tote.

"You better keep that on."

"No, it hinders me."

"What you said a minute ago . . ." he began.

Rebecca smiled nervously. "Yes?"

"It was unrealistic from start to finish."

"So you've given it some thought?" He was silent. She went on in a chatty voice. "Well, so have I. And the way we took to each other, I don't mean at first—what we did—there has to be something there." She tried to look past his expressionless eyes. She saw him searching, asking himself if he believed her.

He hesitated for a moment. "It was like you said. We were thrown together by accident. Just lust."

"I never said just lust!"

"You made me think it. Same thing."

His stubborn tenacity was infuriating, especially since he was so wrong! "Can we agree to discuss it once we're back in Boise? We can meet for coffee or something." She just couldn't let him go out of her life.

"Okay," he said. He didn't go into Boise more than five times a year. Amos did all the grocery shopping. Sometimes business took Parnell out to the regional airport, but he bid contracts from his desk, or the kitchen table in the trailer out behind the the hangar. Everything else got done by phone. Hell. Rebecca had just let him off the hook.

The boys appeared out of the woods from the direction of the temporary latrine. "Molly wants you, Rebecca," Santee yelled. "Her zipper's stuck and she won't let me help. You better hurry. She's afraid a grizzly is gonna get her while her pants are down."

"A grizzly?" She headed into the woods. "No bear in his right mind would come within a mile of me today!"

"Amen to that," she heard Parnell say.

She dealt him a lofty smile over her shoulder. "Isn't it your turn to do breakfast dishes?"

"There really might be grizzlies or brown bears around here," he returned.

"Oh, great!" She took off at a trot.

Parnell stared after her, liking the way she moved. "But, not at this time of year," he muttered sotto voce, pleased with himself.

"What's funny?" Yancy asked.

"Nothing! Get your poncho on before I separate your head from your neck." In Parnell's estimation it was a good threat. In the past days he'd perfected several variations of it to keep the boys in line. But now Yancy just stood there aping him. "You deaf or something? Get with it. We're ready to haul out of here."

"Geez! I hate grown-ups. I hope I stay a kid forever."

"That can be arranged," Parnell said, warming up to a tirade. Being around the kids had given him an anxiety neurosis. If he believed in shrinks—which he didn't—he'd have to spend two years on a couch just to rid himself of it.

Yancy shuffled out of Parnell's reach. "You're an ugly old man."

Ugly didn't bother Parnell but *old* did. "I'm not old."

"You look old. You got wrinkles around your eyes."

"Those are laugh lines."

"You're not laughing now and they're still there."

Parnell scowled which added wrinkles to his brow. He could see Yancy counting them. "Your day's coming, brat. I hope you own a kid just like yourself someday."

Yancy drew himself up. "I am never gonna have any little kids. Intercourse is yukky. And besides, you'd have to do it with a girl."

"Intercourse? Intercourse!" Parnell was shocked. "Where'd you learn words like that?"

"In school."

"If we could spare it, I'd wash your mouth out with soap for lying. You don't learn that in school."

"Yes, we do, in sex education."

"In my day we learned that stuff on the street!"

"Now you have to read it in a book. You learned in olden times."

Parnell made some unpleasant hostile sounds.

"That kind of language indicates a very poor vocabulary," Rebecca said acidly, on approach with Molly in tow. "Yancy, get your poncho on."

Parnell faced Rebecca. First he had to put up with a kid calling him names, now Rebecca was attacking him. "I'll have you know I'm in my prime," he ground out in defense, which made not one whit of sense to Rebecca.

"Well . . . okay," she answered, taken aback.

"It's disgusting. Seven-and eight-year-olds discussing sex."

Rebecca clamped her hands over Molly's ears. "Have you lost your mind? Sex is not a topic for youngsters."

His lips curled in a smirk. "Just goes to show how much you know."

His sarcasm engulfed Rebecca. "You're worse than the kids. You're not happy unless you're stirring up trouble or fighting. I can't take any more! The sooner we part company, the better I'll like it. Direct me to that road."

"My pleasure," he said, bending over in an exaggerated bow.

"You should think twice before you present such a target, Parnell. Somebody might consider it the perfect opportunity to knock some sense into your head."

He snapped straight. "And you should keep your sweater buttoned up, Rebecca. Somebody might consider your display of flesh entrapment. That is, once he has some sense, however gained." Her face closed up. Parnell grinned inwardly. Goading, he thought, did have its compensations.

"YOU SAID A ROAD!" Rebecca wailed accusingly. The lane was narrow and in places wind-swept of snow, so that the dark earth and ruts were visible where the sun shone through a towering overhead foliage.

"It is a road. I didn't say it was the Los Angeles Freeway. What'd you expect?"

"Lines painted down the middle, road signs, cars, a motel, a bath, a telephone—a real road," she said lamely. "Not a path out in the middle of nowhere."

"Some people just can't be pleased," Parnell groused. "It is a real road. It was probably constructed by a lumber company to carry trucks, or maybe a parks department."

"At least it's flat," said Jonesy, dropping down on the verge. "I couldn't crawl over another rock or wade through another inch of snow for a hundred dollars."

"Well . . . ?" said Parnell. "Do you want to stand here jawing and whining or get on with it?"

Pulling Nicholas along, Santee lurched through a drift and stood in the middle of the road. "Which way?"

"Just flip a coin," Rebecca said, dejected.

"We'll keep southeast," Parnell said, and directed Santee left. He started to take Rebecca's arm but stopped himself. Better not take too big a leap of faith, he told himself. "Give me your pack," he offered instead. "It'll free you to help Molly."

It was an offer she couldn't refuse. The makeshift straps were cutting into her shoulders despite her coat.

Parnell watched her face. She was keeping her thoughts to herself. He couldn't read anything into her expression. Maybe he'd gone just a bit overboard, carrying on as he'd been. If he knew for certain just what she'd say, he'd... But suppose she said no? Or just stared at him with those big gray eyes as if he were a candidate for a mental institution?

He tried to tell himself that the law of averages might be on his side. He was due some good luck. On the other hand, who trusted averages? If one believed in statistics, every human on the face of the earth was likely to die twice over of some terrible disease.

If only there was a way he could bring up the future in a roundabout way. After they'd trudged a quarter mile in silence he hit on it.

"Cheer up, Rebecca. You'll be back in Abigail's parlor before you know it. Tucked in front of that great old fireplace."

"I guess so." But the orphanage wasn't where she wanted to spend the rest of her life. Abigail had taken her in as a lost soul, much as she had the children. She didn't feel so lost now—at least in the literal sense. "I

won't stay tucked for long. Abigail's closing the home.
The foundation's out of money."

Every fiber in Parnell's being came alert. "Oh? What
will you do then?"

"Find another job."

The wheels in his head began to spin. He looked at it
from every angle. Yep, he thought. Maybe there was a
way. He'd think it out. "What about the kids?" he said,
pouring sympathy into his voice.

"The state will find them foster homes."

"Poor tykes."

She glanced at him, taking in his profile as he
matched her, step for step, in the crisp snow. "You're
buttering me up for something."

He'd suspected it, but now he knew for sure. She
could read his mind. "I'm not."

"You want me to tell everybody how thoughtful and
wonderfully heroic you've been."

"Hell no!" Despite his protest, pleasing headlines
popped into his head anyway. *Pilot saves social worker
and five orphans.*

"When I came into your office and found you asleep,
I should've turned around and left."

"Then I'd've been out here all by myself."

"Meaning?"

"Meaning?" Meaning! How'd this happen? He circled around it warily. "Well, I want you to know I have
enjoyed your company. Some of the time."

"You sound like a thank-you note with reserva-
tions." She recalled the texture of his skin against her
own when their bodies had been entwined. Recalled the
feeling she'd had of being well loved, secure. And every

step out of the wilderness was one step closer to being separated from him. She felt a dull ache in her heart.

He watched her out of the corner of his eye. "A person doesn't have to get along with someone every minute of the day. It's not possible."

"I couldn't agree with you more, present company included."

When he next glanced at her she was deep in thought. The delicate line of her jaw was tense. She stumbled. He put out his arm steadying her at the waist. When she didn't shrug him off he arranged a scowl on his face to mask his pleasure.

THE ADVANTAGE of following the road, beyond the promise it held out to them, was that they were all in view of one another at all times. Rebecca lagged behind, as did Jonesy, who was suffering terribly with his feet.

It was only when Parnell called for a rest that the tired little party cheered up, they straightened their tortured backs and ignored their sore feet. "On the whole," Rebecca complained, "we're in far worse shape than any time since the crash itself!"

Parnell held up his hand. "No nagging. It's disheartening and will only slow us down."

Rebecca burst into tears of rage and misery. "Why didn't they find us? Why didn't they keep looking?"

Parnell trooped to her side and hunkered down. "Come on, hush," he said softly, brushing gently at the tears on her cheeks. "You've done great. I just pick at you to have something to say. To reassure myself you're still with me. Right now all I'm asking from you is the will to survive a bit longer. You can't lose it now. We're close to getting out of this, I feel it."

The pep talk, along with his gentle manner helped. She nodded. "Okay. But couldn't we have a fire—just a small one?"

"All right. But we can't build one at every rest stop or we'll run out of matches."

While Parnell passed out some of the last malt tablets, Rebecca gathered moss and twigs, piling them at the roadside. The small mound was carefully lighted. They collapsed around it.

"We might as well check ourselves over," Parnell instructed.

Though the rigged pack straps had cut into shoulders, socks were wearing thin and pants were ragged, Jonesy's feet were the worse. He'd lost so much weight that his shoes were now too big. They kept slipping and rubbing his blisters raw. Rebecca peeled his socks away.

"He can have my socks," offered Santee.

"And, mine," Parnell said.

Once the exchange was made, they stumbled off again.

As they plodded on, their spirits lifted. In spite of their aching legs and arms, the walking was keeping them warm and they were making much faster progress than before.

At each bend in the road the anticipation grew that they would round it and come upon a house, a park station, or meet the rescue team.

"Are we nearly there?" begged Molly.

"Where is there?" said Santee.

"We're on a road," Parnell said, reassuring them as they trudged along. "Every mile we cover is one mile closer to somebody."

Rebecca sensed in Parnell an urgency that she didn't share. It was all she could do to coax one foot in front of the other and find voice to encourage the youngsters forward.

Lunch was a frugal affair, prepared right in the middle of the road. In any case, there was nothing left for supper except powdered milk and a handful of malt tablets. Parnell allowed them a longer rest. He spread the thermal foil blanket and the little group huddled together like puppies. Aching and uncomfortable they curled up and were all asleep within five minutes.

An hour later Parnell shook Rebecca awake and made her stand up. "We've got to keep moving."

"I don't know if I can!"

"Just a bit farther."

He wakened the kids. "Let's push on, boys."

They staggered forward. The sun weakened, their shadows grew longer.

They came around a bend; the trees widened out suddenly as if they had been pushed back for the express purpose of revealing a valley of snow-capped hills. A quarter mile farther and the trees engulfed the road once more. Rebecca gasped at the beauty of the panoramic view.

"God's work," she said.

"More like the devil's," Parnell muttered, taking in the sheer drop from the verge of the road. "You kids get back from there! Damn it! That's all we need, one of you to go falling off a mountain."

"Can't be much worse than falling out of the sky," Rebecca retorted.

"Keep moving!" he said. The road narrowed where snow had drifted against the cliff to the left. Parnell glanced up at the wall of snow. The look and shape of the ice sent alarm signals clanging through the back lobes of his brain.

Jonesy hobbled to the edge of the drop and issued an unsuccessful yodel. It came echoing back, reverberating off the mountain.

"Don't do that!" Parnell ordered so softly Rebecca caught his alarm. Her heart skipped a beat.

"What's wrong?"

"I don't know. Maybe nothing. I don't like the way that snow looks."

The late-afternoon sun was bathing the sheer upward slant a pinkish gold. "It's beautiful, though," Rebecca said.

"And dangerous." He yanked Molly off her feet and deposited her on his shoulders.

Down the road well within the shadows of the trees, a movement caught Rebecca's eye. The movement became a man who was waving his arms and shouting.

"Oh!" she cried. "We're found! Parnell! We're found!" Her knees buckled and she sat down.

He grabbed her arm and jerked her to her feet. "Keep moving!"

"It has to be the rescue team!"

But Nicholas, who had God's compensation of keen hearing, puffed, "He's calling us idiots."

A great rumbling sound overtook them. Parnell stopped and stared up the cliff. A great wall of snow seemed to erupt slowly from the top of the escarpment.

Now there were two men shouting at them. Parnell thrust Nicholas into Rebecca's arms. "Run! Everybody, run!"

Santee grabbed Yancy's hand and the two boys sprinted forward.

Parnell shoved at Jonesy so hard the boy lifted from his already loosened shoes.

At first Rebecca only heard the sounds of her tortured breath, the yelps of Nicholas, the thudding of boots pounding, but after a moment a greater sound seemed to burst the very air. Jonesy streaked past her.

The men were coming out of the forest toward them, their faces stricken, hands out. One of them jerked Nicholas from Rebecca. Breathless, sides aching, she collapsed and felt herself being dragged.

Behind her, the noise was as if the world was coming to an end.

She lay on the ground, lungs bursting, and lifted her head.

As it broke entirely away from the earth, the massive wall of snow sent spume shooting into the air. The sun penetrated it causing starbursts of color. Parnell was sprinting hard, Molly bobbing and screaming atop his shoulders.

"Man, he's not gonna make it," came a stunned voice from above her.

Rebecca scrambled to her feet, attempting to lurch forward. Strong arms held her.

The men were yelling encouragement to Parnell.

A huge chunk of ice slammed into his legs. He lost his grip on Molly and she flew through the air and then the miasma of snow swallowed them both.

Rebecca sagged.

It was a full minute before she realized the screaming in her ears was coming from herself. She choked it back.

Another few seconds and there was deep silence.

"They couldn't live through that," Rebecca said, almost inaudible.

"Don't give them up so easily, little lady," a gravelly voice said in an aside as he delegated a crew to begin

searching with an urgency proclaimed by sharp stac-
cato orders.

She looked at the men, a half dozen or more of them
now. "Why couldn't you have come sooner?" she
wailed. "Five minutes sooner?"

The man who had first spoken shook his head, and
after a moment, Rebecca and the boys were ushered
some yards along the road where a caravan was parked
among trucks and oversized snow-and earth-moving
machines.

Dazed, Rebecca let herself be helped into the caravan and seated. Blankets were brought and draped over
their shoulders. Someone brought out a medical kit.
Bruises and scrapes were inspected, cleaned, and
Jonesy's feet were bandaged.

At the periphery of her consciousness Rebecca ab-
sorbed the dialogue directed toward her.

The men worked for a lumber company. They were
opening the road to a camp deep in the forest. The av-
alanche had been man-made, activated by dynamite.
And except for their presence, a perfect "blow." A mug
of hot coffee laced heavily with milk and sugar was
thrust into her hands.

"How'd you get into the forest," asked the crew foreman. "That road hasn't seen any traffic in three weeks."

Rebecca took a sip of the coffee. "Our plane crashed.
I don't know where. We were walking out."

The foreman exhaled. "Dear God in heaven! When?"

Rebecca had to stop and think. "The twelfth. The
morning of the twelfth."

"We have to get you to the authorities. Was
there . . . how many?" He slapped his forehead. "You're

the social worker with the orphans from Idaho aren't you? It was on the news."

Rebecca nodded. "I don't want to leave here until you've found Molly and Captain Stillman. I won't leave."

"Neither will any of us," Santee asserted. "We started together. We want to finish together."

He had said it as well as she herself might have. Rebecca lifted her ashen face and smiled her approval at the boy. Of all the children, he and Molly were the closest to each other.

"We'll give it until dark," said the burly built crew chief. "That's the most I can promise."

Rebecca met his gaze with a jut of jaw and a frosty look in her eyes that betrayed a certain hostility. "We've been through a lot together. We're not leaving without Molly and the captain. We can't."

"Ma'am, you don't understand—"

"It's you who doesn't understand! If it weren't for Captain Stillman none of us would be alive today. And if he's—" She couldn't finish.

"We're not deserting him or Molly," Santee said. "She'd be scared of strangers."

"We'd tell the police you were mean to us," promised Yancy.

"Right," the foreman grunted finally and stepped out of the caravan.

Rebecca heard him yelling for someone to scare up some sandwiches. Her adrenaline spent, she sagged against the plastic cushions. The sandwiches were brought, but she found she couldn't swallow. Nor could she stay snug and warm inside the camper while Molly and Parnell might be—were surely—struggling for their lives. She slipped outside.

SHE STARED OUT at the gathering darkness as she paced up and down the road. She could hear the search party calling out to one another, but she couldn't see them. The air was redolent with the smell of earth. She glanced once at the escarpment from which the wall of snow had been dynamited. It looked bleak and raw and rocky. It looked the way she felt. The fear that kept sweeping over her had settled into a tightness in her throat.

When she heard a commotion coming from far down the mountainside, her heart missed a beat. *Both of them, God!* she prayed. *Please, both of them.*

Santee came racing up to her. "It's Molly," he yelled breathlessly. "She's alive!" Rebecca didn't have the courage to ask about Parnell. It would be too much like bargaining with God.

Molly was more than alive. She was hoarse and furious. Inside the caravan Rebecca gathered the child into her arms. The tumbling snow had rocketed Molly into a small gully out of which she couldn't climb. She had yelled until her throat hurt she said.

"I didn't like it. I was by myself and I thought a bear was gonna get me and my clothes are all torn up and I went and wet my pants, but I didn't mean to."

Rebecca brushed hair back off the child's forehead. "It's all right sweetheart. We'll get you—" She looked up into the cratered face of the man who'd thrust Molly into her arms. "Thank you."

He left to rejoin the search for Parnell. Santee hovered. Reluctantly Rebecca relinquished Molly into his care; she could see he needed to touch the girl. To make the rescue of her real. As she needed to see and touch Parnell. She went back to pacing the road.

The moon came up, but was soon hidden by cloud, only a faint luminosity lingering. The heavy earth-and snow-moving equipment loomed up, dark shadows whose shapes seemed imbued with life. The torches and flashlights of the searchers were like pinpricks in the distance. They had sticks and were poking them deep into the snow.

The crew foreman approached her. Rebecca sensed what he was going to tell her. He wanted to stop the search. Night was hard on them, the wind had come up. It was cold down on the slope with no protection. He was thinking of his men. But she had to think of Parnell. If he were under the snow, what chance did he have of lasting until morning. When the foreman lifted the Coleman lamp it illuminated the tightness of her lips, the strained look in her eyes. She had death looking over her shoulder, she wasn't about to give in.

"If you stop now, you'd be killing him!" she shouted, depriving the man of a soft approach, the coaxing she was certain he'd attempt.

He hesitated. "Ma'am, you don't seem to realize, it was a miracle we found the girl. I've sent one of the boys to notify the authorities. We don't have a chance in hell now of finding your friend, at least—not alive."

"He's alive! He's been through worse! He's flown into the eye of hurricanes and survived; he's landed on aircraft carriers in twenty-foot seas; he's done belly landings and crashed into a corn field! Don't tell me he's dead!"

The man tried to put his arm round her. "You're upset. You have a right to be, considering—"

Rebecca jerked away. "Give me that lamp! I'll search for him myself!"

"For God's sake, lady—"

The shouting came from below them on the slope. Rebecca froze. "What'd he say?" she whispered.

Then she heard it clearly, the words echoing into dark. "We found him! He's breathing!"

Rebecca snatched at the foreman's coat. "There!" she said triumphantly. "You see?" Then she crumpled to the ground and sat there, hugging her knees, rocking, crying.

"The reason I like this job," the man said succinctly, "is because there ain't a woman within forty miles on any given day." He bent down and helped Rebecca to her feet, surprised to find that she was smiling at him through her tears.

"I know a man who holds those exact same sentiments."

The foreman's name was Edwin Salter, called Salty by friend and foe alike. The lamp dangled in his hand, the upward glow illuminating Rebecca's face which seemed bloodless to him. Her eyes were gleaming and feverish. "Pull yourself together," he said, thinking how sad it was that after all she'd been through, she had utterly lost all her senses.

13

MOLLY CIRCLED AND DANCED around Rebecca like an excited puppy. "Is any of that mail for me?"

"We'll see."

"Pour it out on the table," said Abigail. "We'll sort it before supper."

"You're as bad as Molly," Rebecca chided.

The charming old wreck of a woman grinned and put her arms about Molly. "What're the most famous words in our world?"

"'Has Santa Claus come yet?'" Molly responded, collapsing into a welter of giggles.

"We ought to invite that reporter for dinner sometime," Abigail mused. "The story she wrote and photos she took sure wrung a lot of hearts."

Rebecca shook her head. Abigail had a tough dryness, a voluble energy, an inconsequent loquacity, a warm-hearted kindness illumined by a shrewdness one seldom gave the frail woman credit for. And all of that was dedicated toward the children's benefit, but still...

"Doesn't it bother you to keep exploiting the situation, the children?" she asked.

Abigail snorted. "Bother me? Where, my young friend, is your sense of justice? Here we were, the Foundation, out of money, trying to place the children in God knows what kind of homes and along comes this heavensent opportunity.... Look at all these letters!

Most of them containing checks. There's money for Nicholas to have eye surgery. Would you deny him the chance to see? Money for Molly to have her feet straightened. Money to buy food, pay the fuel bill. And money left over for trust funds for the kids. Every single one of them. College! Do realize what kind of future—"

"I know, but—" Rebecca was remembering the frenzy when they had deplaned in Boise, the rush of flash bulbs going off, cameras, microphones thrust into their faces, the questions screamed from every direction. She was remembering with mortification the photo of herself, too. Hair awry, eyes swollen, clothes bedraggled. She'd been carrying Molly, and the enterprising reporter had gone behind her back and asked Molly how they had celebrated Christmas in the wild.

Molly's shocked expression, the now famous words, had been flashed to television stations across the country.

It had been the day after Christmas. The idea that the orphans had missed Christmas had grabbed a nation by its heart and opened wallets when most people were still in the afterglow of a holiday spirit.

Offers to adopt the children had poured in. But Abigail was finding fault with each and every prospective parent. The Tynan Foundation could now afford to be choosy. After all, Abigail said over and over, what with their trust funds being established, it was as if the children would be taking dowries into their new homes. One couldn't be too careful.

Not to mention more practical matters. According to the Indian Child Welfare Act, Santee's adoption would have to be approved by Tribal Council. That sometimes took years. Nor could Abigail consider separating Molly and Santee. Santee would most assuredly have to be on hand to cheer Molly on during the girl's foot surgery next summer.

Nicholas was scheduled for cornea transplants. Abigail was reserving for herself the joy of showing the boy the wonders of the world. And it wouldn't be fair would it, to send Jonesy and Yancy out of the bosom of the Tynan family while all these exciting things were going on?

"I do wish you would give an interview," Abigail said, momentarily drawing Rebecca out of her thoughts.

"The children have said it all. I'd be boring."

Parnell wasn't giving any interviews, either. He was refusing on the grounds of the ongoing investigation by the Federal Aviation Agency and the postal inspectors. For a time, he had hidden behind a hospital gown.

He'd been unconscious when the rescuers had brought him up to the camp. She had neither seen nor heard from him since he'd been whisked off in an ambulance. She knew only what she'd read in the papers. He'd suffered a dislocated shoulder, some terrible bruising. But he'd been out of the hospital for four days now. Television cameras had recorded his discharge.

He'd had plenty of time to call her and hadn't. She had a mental list of reasons why he had not.

He was busy filling out forms for insurance to replace his plane.

The FAA investigators were grilling him.

The postal inspectors had him in jail for losing the mail, opening the box of apples.

The press was sitting on his doorstep and he couldn't escape.

He had amnesia and didn't recall that she even existed.

His telephone had been disconnected.

With her very bright, sharp eyes Abigail was absorbing every expression flitting across Rebecca's face. "Molly, my sweet," she said. "I'm going to leave you the job of sorting the mail. Put all the ones with your name into a pile by itself. I'll help you open them later." She then took Rebecca's arm. "Come along, I think it's time you and I had a little talk. Let's have tea by the fire in the parlor."

The room was full of the scent of chrysanthemums, splashed with colorful poinsettias and a towering Christmas tree fully lit—a gift from an anonymous donor.

The position of the furniture had not been changed in forty years. The old sofas and chairs were elegant, shabby and comfortable. In another part of the old farmhouse was a den which held the television. The parlor's focus was a grand stone fireplace.

"I've always liked this room," said Abigail as she poured and passed Rebecca the delicate china cup. "It's just always seemed a room in which one could air one's problems, see them in a truer light."

"I don't have a problem," Rebecca said, regretting at once the telltale sharpness of her tone.

"My dear, Parnell Stillman is most assuredly a problem. You forget. I've known the boy since he was a teenager. I admit there was that gap of time when he was in the Navy, but his Uncle Henry talked of him often."

"I'm sure I haven't given you any indication—"

The elderly woman held up a care-worn hand. "Rebecca dear, you've spoken volumes by omission. Every time his name is mentioned on the news, you fly to the television. When the telephone rings, you tense, you hover as I speak. So distracting. You read and reread everything printed about him, then you look off into space.

"I may be old, but my eyes and ears are as sharp as they've ever been. You're in a funk. At first I put it down to the terrible ordeal you've suffered. But as I listen more and more to the children, I realize that though there was extreme difficulty and hardship, there was also a sense of adventure. Santee can barely keep his mouth shut. Exactly opposite the way he'd been for months. That boy was almost a mute, except when it came to Molly. Well, that's neither here nor there. My point is, you've met your match in Parnell."

"That doesn't mean—"

"Pooh. You're in love with him. The Stillmans have always been a rogue species. Parnell's a bit of a mongrel. So was his Uncle Henry." There was a note of affection in her voice. The words almost an endearment. "That appeals to a woman. It most assuredly appealed to me. Getting one of them to marry is the problem."

Rebecca sank deeper into the overstuffed chair and with a weak smile, gave up all pretense. "What can I do?"

"I've invited him to supper."

An electric force shot through Rebecca. "He's accepted?"

"He could hardly refuse. After all, I did hire him to fly all of you to San Francisco. The detour was not to my liking. I suffered terrible bouts of depression. Not to mention how frightened I was for all of you. I never thought you dead, but I did imagine you maimed and suffering. He owes me."

"When?"

"Tonight. I didn't think it would be too troublesome, what with having the funds to recall the cook—"

Rebecca put down the tea cup with a clatter. "Oh!"

"My dear," Abigail said to Rebecca's departing back, "you must remember to be careful with that china. It was my grandmother's, you know. Irreplaceable."

SHE HAD TO LOOK HER BEST, smell wonderful, wear her frilliest underwear. Bathe and shampoo her hair. Those things accomplished, she demolished her closet. The ivory sweater dress, she decided. But the lack of color made her look drab. Anyway, it was too formal. She settled finally on a burgundy cashmere sweater with matching slacks. Not too much makeup. Mascara on her lashes and the barest hint of blush.

She knew he had arrived when she heard the excited squeals and shrieks of the children. The tapping on her bedroom door made perspiration break out on her palms.

"Rebecca?" came Abigail's voice. "Our dinner guest is here."

"I'm just coming," she said, and grabbed a tissue, drying her palms.

They were all gathered in the parlor. A log had been added to the fire. The Christmas-tree lights sparkled. The children were sprawled in chairs, on the sofa, on the floor.

Parnell was standing near the fire, a drink in his hand. He glanced up as she entered the room. Their eyes met.

Suddenly Rebecca couldn't swallow, couldn't breathe properly. She had absolutely no idea what he felt for her anymore.

"Hello," she said softly and her eyes took him in. She had spent hours going over the contours of his face in her mind, impressing it into her memory so she could always retrace it. It was different now. He had shaved. The beard gone, but a thick dark mustache held forth over the sensual curve of his mouth. He wore a suit and tie, cuffs perfectly shot. He lifted his drink in greeting, as if he, too, was at a loss for words.

"You two have met," Abigail said into the silence.

Thus prompted, Parnell found his voice. "How are you, Rebecca?"

"Fine, thank you."

"What wonderfully scintillating conversation," Abigail scoffed in disgust.

"Usually they fight," put in Jonesy.

Rebecca saw Parnell flinch then. She could see that his eyes were as bright as hers felt. She was afraid to say anything. It was useless to try to make small talk anyway, she thought, when the greater question loomed and filled her with tension. She sank down on the arm of a chair occupied by Santee, suddenly too weak to stand.

"Come along to the dinner table, children," Abigail said. "Let's leave these two to become reacquainted."

Rebecca protested. "I thought—"

"You got me over here on the pretense of dinner," Parnell said, his dark eyes glinting wildly, and his gaze touching on everyone in the room except Rebecca.

"I'm still indulging the children's appetites," Abigail returned airily. "It's hot dogs with chili for them. We adults are having rare roast beef. I'll send the cook for you. Thirty minutes."

She herded the children out of the parlor, down the wide hall and to the back of the house.

"Well," Rebecca said.

"I need a drink," Parnell said.

"You have one in your hand."

"Refill, then." He loosened his tie with a savage jerk. "Am I such awful company that—"

He ran his fingers through his hair, disheveling it. Rebecca couldn't take her eyes from him. Closer inspection revealed his cuff links didn't match, the collar button beneath the tie knot was missing. He was almost the familiar Parnell she knew and loved.

"You're not awful company. What made you think that? It's—you look beautiful. I knew you would. I always thought of you as silk, imagined you—" Hell! He wasn't about to say that.

"You did?" When he stayed mute, she went on, found a safer topic. "How's your shoulder?"

He flexed beneath the suit jacket. "A little sore, not enough to keep me from work."

"How is it? Work? The airfield?"

"Paperwork has me snowed under. Twenty-five different forms to fill out. I have depositions running out my ears. Don't think I'll ever wreck a plane again."

Rebecca took a deep breath. "Could you use some help?"

"You?"

She nodded.

He looked at her for a long moment, then shook his head. "I don't think it's the kind of job you'd like. No excitement."

Rebecca felt her heart seize up. He didn't mean doing office work. He meant in his life! "If you'll excuse me," she said utterly calm, "I'll just go see if Abigail needs—"

"Wait!" He moved across the room to her, grabbed her arm. Touching her sent a jolt to his head. He had promised himself he wouldn't get near her. Now he was breathing in the scent of her, his nerve endings recording the feel of her skin. "Rebecca..." His voice cracked, both his arms went around her.

She bent her head, let it rest on his chest, doing nothing more than absorbing the essence of him, afraid to move, to speak lest she awake and find herself only dreaming.

"Damn! But I've missed you. I've been feeling as if I left a part of me back in those woods."

"Why didn't you call me, you sorry lout?"

"Why didn't you come to the hospital?"

"I was afraid to."

"Afraid? You? Of what?"

"I thought you might not want to see me. What we did, the circumstances..."

"Same here," he said. He bent his head, nuzzled her ear, her brow. "You smell good enough to..." His libido was in a frenzy. "Let's get out here!"

He pulled her along, stopping in the foyer only long enough to grab his overcoat, a wrap for her.

ABIGAIL HEARD the front door slam, heard the heavy motor of Parnell's truck chug to life. She hurried into the foyer, peered out the window.

"A perfectly good roast gone to waste," she said with a sigh. Then she began to think of all the publicity a wedding between the two would garner. Molly as flower girl, Santee as best man. And there was that lovely offer from that magazine tucked at the back of her desk drawer. Not that Rebecca and Parnell would agree. Therefore, she wouldn't ask!

Abigail, my dear, she chided herself, *you're a nasty, interfering old fool. Make that an old avaricious romantic fool,* she amended. A twinge of guilt weighed upon her thin shoulders as she returned to the kitchen. She looked about for some small penance with which to assuage her conscience.

"Pass the mustard, Santee," she said. "I think I'll try one of those dreadful wieners."

14

HE WAS STROKING her hair, her face, kissing her neck, her ears, her lips, as though he would starve without her. He hadn't let her go since they entered his trailer. He had led her to the bedroom, turned on a lamp and undressed her.

"I knew it would be like this," Parnell said. "I kept dreaming how it would be in a bed, not having to worry about anyone listening." He drew his hand down from her shoulder to her thigh. "You've gained back some weight."

"Not romantic," Rebecca murmured. She reached up and traced his dimples. "I never knew you had these."

"I keep 'em in reserve. When all else fails...."

"Did you think you were going to?"

"I didn't know what to think."

"Now you do?"

"I only know I've been miserable."

That seemed about as far as he meant to take it. He was doing things to her with the tips of his fingers, making it hard for her to concentrate beyond the excitement, the swelling in her body.

Her eyes feasted on his muscular arms, the wide shoulders, the narrow hips, savoring him piece by piece. Against her pelvis his erection pulsated with a life of its own. She ran her fingers over the throbbing vein.

Parnell moaned, bruising her lips with furious kisses. Her lips were as hungry as his. Rebecca ached with happiness. This was how it would be between them forever, she thought.

She hadn't known what to actually expect after the wild drive out to the airfield. He hadn't told her that he loved her. She hadn't told him, either. But then, in that first rush, that first desperateness, the only thing that had seemed important was to be in each other's arms, to satisfy the deep visceral craving.

As his hands played over her, Parnell watched her face with pleasure. He felt so drawn to her, as if she were a refuge where he belonged.

"Do turn off the light," she begged.

"Not a chance." He flicked his tongue in the hollow of her neck, felt the pulse beating fast and hard.

"At least close your eyes."

"Can't. I'm afraid you'll disappear. I have to keep my hands on you. I have to . . . Damn! I've never *needed* anyone so much!"

He moved atop her then, spreading her legs with his knees, but pushed into her slowly, deliberately giving her time to feel him inside her, as if entreating her to surrender more of herself. When she felt him barely inside her, she held her body taut and poised. Their hands and mouths stroked, touched, searched. He burrowed his head between her breasts, his mouth lingering on one nipple, pulling in and releasing. Then he was greedily penetrating her thighs. "Hold me, Rebecca," he whispered as he thrust deep into her. "Hold me."

"PARNELL, LET ME UP. I have to get dressed." There was little conviction in her voice, she felt relaxed and dreamy.

He draped a terry robe about her shoulders. "Hate like hell to have you covered up, but here—put this on."

"I can't go back to the orphanage wearing your robe."

"I want you to stay here. You're kidnapped."

She drew a shaky breath. "Don't joke." But she slipped into the robe and belted it.

"What do you think of the trailer?"

"All I've seen is the bedroom. The bed's nice."

He ushered her from room to room until the tour ended in the surprisingly roomy kitchen. "Well? What do you think?"

"It's bigger than I expected. Cleaner, too. Considering what your office looks like."

"This is where I live! You wouldn't expect me to wallow in dirt."

"Hate to tell you, but I did expect it." He was leading up to that wonderful something—marriage. She couldn't bear him dragging it out, teasing her. "Give me a hint. Why do you want my opinion?"

He hesitated. "Did you mean it—your offer to help with my paperwork?"

Casually, she pulled back a curtain, gazed out the window. Halos surrounded the vapor lights on the airstrip. All else was dark. "Of course. The Foundation has an unexpected cash flow now. Abigail is looking for more help. She can replace me. I can still help her out, though, on a volunteer basis."

"That's great. I need a bookkeeper in the worst—"

She whirled to face him, her gray eyes blazing. "Bookkeeper? *Bookkeeper?* That's why you dragged me here?"

"You know that's not the only reason—"

"Right! You wanted a little on the side! Well, no thank you!"

"Wait a minute!"

"No! You wait. You need a bookkeeper and a live-in piece of flesh, too? What were you going to offer me? Bedroom gymnastics between accounts receivable and payable? Just to sweeten the offer?"

"I know what you want! You want to tie me into knots. Give me ulcers. Turn me into a wimp. 'Do this, honey. Do that, honey.' I'm not a man to rush into things!"

"Oh, I can think of any number of names to call you besides 'honey.' Like, lowlife, two-faced, vulture—"

"Hold on! Are you perfect? Look at the way your nose is going up."

"There's a bad smell in here. Excuse me, I have to get my clothes on."

THE TELEPHONE BEGAN RINGING at two o'clock in the morning. Not yet able to sleep, Rebecca hurried to answer it. Abigail switched on the hall light.

"We both know who that is," the old woman said. "For heaven's sake, answer it before he wakes the whole house!"

"It's me," said Parnell, his voice throaty, irritable. "I can't sleep."

"So you want to keep the rest of the world awake?"

"We're not going to let the sun set on our little differences, are we?"

"The sun's been down for hours."

"I'm not giving up wanton women and lost weekends for this kind of misery."

"What wanton women?"

"Don't you want to know why I can't sleep?"

"I couldn't care less."

"My pillow smells like your shampoo. My sheets smell like your perfume. It's driving me crazy."

"I'm surprised your stomach doesn't hurt."

"It does. I ache all over. I wish you could see what else aches."

Rebecca remained silent, the telephone clenched in her hand, pressed to her ear.

"Rebecca?"

"I'm listening."

"I can't live without you."

Her legs were suddenly weak, air disappeared from her lungs. "You can't?"

Parnell felt the collapse of his vocal cords. The most important words he'd ever have to speak in his life and he couldn't get them up. He inhaled, spinning words out in a rush on the exhale. "Damn it! I love you." There was such silence from Rebecca it scared him. "Did you hear me?"

"Yes. Was there something else?"

"Else? What else could there—oh." His heart was pounding in his ears. His eyes closed for a moment, his breath stopped, he was sure he had died. "You want to—" his voice faded "—get married?"

"Yes."

He held the receiver away from his ear and stared at it. "Did you say yes?"

"A thousand times—yes!"

Parnell sighed heavily. "That's all right, then."

"Very much all right," Rebecca whispered.

"I can be there in forty-five minutes," Parnell said, all hope.

"There's only the sofa."

"Better Abigail's sofa with you nearby than my bed without you."

ABIGAIL WOULDN'T STAND for the wedding to be held in the office of the justice of the peace. "I feel responsible. We'll have the wedding here in the parlor. I'm sure my old friend, Judge Stanley will preside. Besides, you can't leave out the kids. They were part and parcel of the whole affair."

Parnell looked at her. "No reporters, Abigail. I know how your sly mind works. I won't have you turn this into a circus."

"Just a photographer? You'll want pictures, won't you?"

"Of course we will," Rebecca agreed, slipping her arm through Parnell's.

THE BRIEF CEREMONY was over. Parnell looked dazed. Rebecca smiled. "That wasn't so bad was it?"

"I hope not. It's for the rest of my life."

"Mine, too."

His arm snaked about her waist possessively. "Let's go somewhere. I want to get a head start on what grooms do on their wedding night."

"What's that?" asked Jonesy. He, as did all of the boys looked trim and neat in their new suits.

"You'll grow up and find out one day," Parnell said. "Unless you keep eavesdroping, in which case, you'll be dead."

"Time to cut the cake," Abigail announced, ushering the bride and groom into the dining room. The cake was cut, champagne poured, pictures taken, with Molly somehow managing to be in every shot.

"Okay. It's officially over. Let's go," Parnell said.

"Don't be in such a hurry," Abigail admonished. "I haven't given you your wedding present. I've been saving it for a surprise." She handed Parnell a thick envelope.

"I can't accept any of the loot you've been dragging in."

"Don't be nasty, dear boy. Open it."

"Parnell!" Rebecca breathed looking over his shoulder. "Those are airline tickets."

"To Hawaii," put in Abigail.

"What's the catch?" Parnell asked, scouring the lace-draped Abigail.

"Don't be so suspicious. Your plane leaves in two hours."

"We can't—"

"We can!" Rebecca put in. "You've already arranged for four days away from the airfield. And I'm packed."

"So is Parnell." Abigail beamed. "I had Amos pack for him. The suitcase is in the hall closet."

"Oh, Parnell! Say, yes!" Rebecca pleaded. "Just think. Beaches, sun—look out the window and tell me no."

Outside it was snowing lightly. White flakes drifting lazily downward. Some of the flakes settled briefly on the windows, sticking for an instant before the warmth from inside penetrated, melting them.

"All right, you win."

"I have it all planned," said Abigail. "The children and I will see you off at the airport."

"Why do I feel I'm being taken?" muttered Parnell.

Judge Stanley pounded him on his back. "Because you just got married, my boy. The feeling never goes away."

At the airport the wedding group drew a crowd when the photographer began snapping pictures of the kids throwing rice and confetti at the newlyweds. Mortified, Parnell sought and received permission to board the plane early. He pushed Rebecca to the last row of seats in the plane. "Finally!" he exhaled.

"It was a lovely wedding," Rebecca said, putting her head on his shoulder.

Parnell stifled a yawn. "I think the champagne has made me sleepy."

Rebecca pressed her lips to his ear. "Close your eyes and rest if you like. I won't mind."

"You won't think I'm a bore?"

"Darling, you're many things, but never boring. No, I'll just consider you're getting rested for a late-night walk on the beach. I'm excited. It'll be so romantic. The moon, blue waters, waves lapping."

Parnell gave her a lazy grin. "Late tonight will be romantic, but I sure as hell am not spending my wedding night on a sand dune. And if you don't let me close my eyes for a minute, if you keep talking, we're gonna have to get off this plane and—"

Rebecca brushed confetti from his jacket. "Go to sleep."

While the rest of the passengers boarded, Rebecca watched Parnell and daydreamed. Once they arrived on the island, they'd have to buy swimsuits. She could almost feel the goodness of the sun on her body. Parnell stirred when the plane took off, but once safely aloft, his eyes closed again. Rebecca passed time reading a magazine and staring out the window. It was not unpleasant. The knowledge that she was Mrs. Parnell Stillman warmed her as much as she imagined the sun soon would.

"Hi," said a small voice.

Rebecca looked across Parnell and stared aghast. "What are you doing on this plane?"

Molly grinned. "We're in first class."

Parnell opened his eyes and glared at Molly. The photographer walked up and snapped their pictures. "Perfect," she said.

"HOW CAN YOU BE SO CALM!" roared Parnell. "The sly old biddie tricked us! Of course we'll have the wedding here," he mimicked. "Of course, no press. Just a photographer. You do want pictures? She *sold* us!"

Rebecca went to the window of their hotel room and stared out. A golden moon traced a path on the blue Pacific, lacy waves curled onto the beach. The first night of her honeymoon! "Are you going to spend all night raging like a bull? I can think of something far more interesting to do. And anyway, Abigail had our best interest at heart. She finagled us a free honeymoon, didn't she? Had you thought of Hawaii? We were going to spend four days cooped up in a Holiday Inn."

"Free? She sold us and the kids as an exclusive! That's where the money came from. I should've guessed. And did you hear what Molly said? 'The captain took off all his clothes and went in the lake and hurt his fanny and Rebecca had to put medicine all over him without his clothes on!' What are people going to think! Our pictures are going to be plastered all— What're you doing?"

"I'm taking off my clothes."

"That chicken-necked old crone kept sneaking up behind me ordering me to restrain myself, keep my hands off you in front of the kids. As if I'm not respectable. To think I just let that go by without a word."

"Of course you're respectable," Rebecca said soothingly.

"Some honeymoon. A clutch of brats and a photographer following us everywhere."

"They're three floors below. You're not going to be-grudge them a few days of sun and sand, are you? They deserve a bit of fun, too. Abigail had to go to great lengths to get permission for them to miss school."

Her dress fell at her feet. She was a mass of cream-colored lace, sheer fabric, glowing skin. Her smile was a smile of complete adoration.

"My permission is the one she should've sought."

"You wouldn't have given it. And you always find twenty-five different ways to argue a point."

"Then how come I never win?"

She began to loosen his tie. "You looked so dashing at the wedding. I'll bet the photos of you will make the cover. I'll be the envy of every woman in America." Her hands slid down his chest.

Parnell began to bask in pleasant sensations to which he tried not to give a name. "I'm never going to win an argument with you," he said. "Your tactics are too dis-tracting. What was I saying?"

"You had to restrain yourself."

She stood before him naked, solemn and clear-eyed. His wife. His woman. Offering herself wholly and without conditions.

"Shall I put my clothes back on?" she asked.

He reached out and touched her smooth sleek body, circled her waist with his fingers and drew her close. "Nope, if this is the way I'm bested, I can probably bear up."

His lips went to her breast, his teeth gently touching her nipple. In the sweet taste of her flesh all else was forgotten.

At length he said, "I just want to lose myself in you."

Rebecca's arms enveloped him.

"That's all right, then," she said and gave herself up to being possessed.

Harlequin Temptation

COMING NEXT MONTH

#209 WILDE 'N' WONDERFUL JoAnn Ross

During a summer on the road Sara McBride let Darius Wilde research her life-style—but she didn't have to like it! He had obviously set his sights on her as a lifetime travel companion, and *that* wasn't part of the deal....

#210 KEEPSAKES Madeline Harper

For Nora Chase, the customer was always right— that was what kept her personalized shopping service thriving. And David Sommer was one sexy customer who had his heart set on the ultimate gift: Nora.

#211 FOXY LADY Marion Smith Collins

Could a flamboyant nightclub singer with a teenage son relate to a conservative anthropology professor with a teenage daughter? Dani and Hamp soon discovered that the answer was a resounding and passionate "yes!"

#212 CAUSE FOR CELEBRATION Gina Wilkins

Overwhelmed by work, theme-party coordinator Merry James breathed a sigh of relief at the appearance of her supposed temporary secretary, Grant Bryant. But soon she suspected that his steamy glances meant he had more on his mind that typing and filing....

Temptation

TEMPTATION WILL BE
EVEN HARDER TO RESIST...

In September, Temptation is presenting a sophisticated new
face to the world. A fresh look that truly brings Harlequin's
most intimate romances into focus.

What's more, all-time favorite authors Barbara Delinsky, Rita
Clay Estrada, Jayne Ann Krentz and Vicki Lewis Thompson
will join forces to help us celebrate. The result? A very special
quartet of Temptations...

- **Four striking covers**
- **Four stellar authors**
- **Four sensual love stories**
- **Four variations on one spellbinding theme**

All in one great month! Give in to Temptation in September.

TDESIGN-1